ON THE REKILL

"Van Dhoc's outside, Buckman. He's here." Leeming's voice was so brittle he was not sure the horrified Buckman could hear him. "Sorry. He can only have one of us. I'm also owed a debt."

Leeming leaned over, grasped the M40 and fired.

A burst of six shells sliced down the front of Buckman's body with such unexpected recoil that Leeming dropped the gun.

Buckman, flattened against the wall, stood there dead for five seconds, the features of his face locked in a scream of incomprehension before he collapsed slowly forward, first onto his knees and then heavily forward onto his face.

Leeming sat there, fought for his consciousness and the reality of Van Dhoc . . .

REKILL

Ian Kennedy Martin

BALLANTINE BOOKS • NEW YORK

Copyright © 1977 by Ian Kennedy Martin

Library of Congress Catalog Card Number: 77-7646

ISBN 0-345-27299-4

This edition published by arrangement with G.P. Putnam's Sons

Manufactured in the United States of America

First Ballantine Books Edition: November 1978

1

THE BROKEN DIRT TRACK headed ruler-straight across the flat farm country of Kansas. It was December, the landscape empty, the activity of the harvest long gone. The earth, still traced with the ash of stubble burning, looked dead. It was five-thirteen, the day cold, and the motionless puffball clouds above threatening nothing.

The truck came from the direction of Newtown. It was a '66 Chevy pickup blistered with rust. It had neither passengers nor goods in the back. The driver wore a pair of cheap Polaroids to view the gray day. He took little action to avoid the potholes—but then he had no reason to preserve the truck. All he needed it for was to transport him the twenty-four miles from Newtown out to the Holby place, then back to Newtown. He'd stolen the Chevy two hours before.

He'd been on U.S. Highway 64, turned off that on to 196. Now he was on the local road which led across the top of Whitewater to some isolated farms. The first of these was the Holby lot.

The man in the bucking vehicle studied the lay of the land carefully. He was a stranger. It was his first time in Kansas. He came from another country, another continent. But he had been a farmer in his time, before the nightmare had overtaken him. He knew how rich this soil was, fallow now in winter, but soon to produce the finest cereal crops in the world. His eyes flickered across the wide acres to the flat horizon, but he was not really speculating about how excellent was this land or how lucky those who owned it, he was looking for figures and threat. By now they would be after him and he knew well the way these people, this nation, dealt with enemies, its encyclopedic approach to the science of death. His eyes searched the skies for Huey helicopters, the ground for M-114 armored personnel carriers, though he realized that was going too far. But still he must continually remind himself he was at war. It was the same war and exactly the same enemy.

He drove on, his mind now concentrating on the mechanics of the task ahead, a concentration so acute that he began to lose a sense of time. Suddenly he saw on the horizon the low house and outbuildings. They were screened by a windbreak of beech trees. The farmhouse was not much of a structure for the headquarters of a three-thousand-acre spread. If the man driving the truck had talked to other farmers in the area they would have been quick to volunteer that old man Holby, who'd cleared this land and built the farm from nothing, had been quite a character, died at ninety, never spent a cent, taught his son that ostentation was for fools, and for every five good farming years there were two bad and that's when you had to have savings because the banks always let you down.

The house wasn't typical of the area. Bleached timber built with supporting brick end-walls, it was flimsy for the locality's winters. It was more like a Deep South farmhouse—old man Holby had come from the South. It was a straight lay of eight rooms, with only a single item to distinguish front from rear. Young Mrs. Holby had once had a Mexican couple and the man had built a rock garden and some bean frames back of the kitchen door. The main outbuildings for the farm were visible east a quarter of a mile away, clustered around an artesian well which had dried out. This had been the original site of the farm forty years ago.

The man in the Polaroids didn't drive the Chevy up to the house, although he knew that at this time of day there'd be no one there. He turned the truck right and headed across a flat earth area with a basketball post, past a shed and on a dozen yards, to pull up behind the screen of beeches.

He turned off the ignition, stepped down from the truck and stood there a second, motionless, testing for any sound from the farmhouse denying his calculation that he was alone. He knew it would be half an hour before Mrs. Holby came back from meeting the school bus with her six-year-old boy and her seven-year-old daughter. The man had once had two children. If they'd lived they would now be roughly the same ages as the Holby kids.

There was an outhouse fifty feet from the east side of the house, an all-purpose shed containing a dismembered Harley Davidson, an abandoned DIY workshop, and four Yale-locked freezers. The driver went around to the back of the Chevy truck and pulled out the two purchases he'd made in Newtown. The first was a coil of rope. He'd gotten the vocabulary wrong, asked in the hardware store for "string" and had received string, and then pointed out to the man a bale of rope and said that was what he wanted. He knew that man would remember him, but he supposed it didn't matter. He was learning this was a large country, America, and every airport meant escape.

The second purchase was a ten-gallon white plastic barrel with a screw-top cap. He'd picked that up at the same Newtown store, then carried it to the parking lot where he'd stolen the truck. Then he'd driven to a Texaco garage. There was a black man on the pumps who said he couldn't fill the barrel because it wasn't marked for gas. The argument was settled with a ten-dollar bill, seven dollars for the gas, the rest a tip.

He lifted the barrel off the truck and carried it across the scratch-earth yard to the four-freezer shed. He pulled open the door, stepped inside, and put the barrel down, then returned to the truck, picked up the rope, went around to the front seat and extracted the Walther PPK9 automatic from where he'd jammed it between the swabs of the front bench seat. He went back to the shed, but didn't go inside.

He got down on his knees on the earth and bowed toward the house. He had lived on this farm unknown to its owners for the last five days. He had slept in the freezer-shed at night, watched the comings and goings, the household routine, from the windbreak during the day. He knew about the camera. That didn't worry him. He had seen those cameras before in his own country. Provided he avoided the angle of view, which was simple, it was no danger. And by the time the camera spotted him it would be too late.

He knelt and prayed. He knew he had a little time before the Ford Limited returned. This prayer interval had been part of his plans. First prayer, then the woman and the two children would return; then, around six o'clock, Holby would get back from the farm office in the Newtown Cooperative where he sat over the forms and order books, doing the winter's business.

The man started his silent prayers. He was a Cao Daist. Cao Dai, the Supreme Being, had been revealed in the early twenties by the spiritualist Ngo Van Chieu to have been the founder of Confucianism, Taoism, Buddhism and Christianity, each based on the customs and mores of the race destined to receive each of these religions. The man on his knees outside this farmhouse in Whitewater, Kansas, was both Cao Daist and communist, an apparent paradox but as possible to reconcile as the contradictions apparent in both the religion and the creed. The man prayed for the success of his mission, for the righting of all universal wrongs, for the memory of the dead of recent events, for the many dead. Then he prayed for his children who had returned to the harmony of the universe. Lastly he prayed for himself, prayed for the Supreme Being to give him help and aid in the immanence of events.

He had become so involved in his prayers that it was with a shock that he heard the sound of the approaching station wagon, then saw it pinpointed by its dust trails a mile away. He looked at his watch. He had been kneeling for forty minutes. He stood up. He was a little shaky on his legs for a few seconds, then he moved back into the shelter of the shed.

The Ford arrived turning into the rear yard, braking with a slight slip of tires on the dry dust. The children spilled out. They seemed to be arguing angrily with each other. Then the girl started chasing the boy into the farmhouse. The woman got out of the car and called after them. She had a task for them to do, but the man did not know enough English to understand the last order she was to give and the last the children were to receive. He waited until she was halfway between the parked car and the farmhouse, then he stepped out of the shed and started to walk after her.

She heard his footsteps and turned. He pointed the Walther down and fired one shot and saw her left kneecap split open like a small paper bag of blood and bone. She went over backward with a scream. Now she could not run away. He would kill her later in front of her husband. The shattered knee was simply to immobilize her. "Capping," the U.S. troops had called it. Those troops had done a lot of "capping."

The children had run back out of the house, drawn by the scream. He walked toward them with the gun raised. They looked from him to their mother expressionless, uncomprehending, maybe for them this was some weird variation on a favorite TV show. He shot them both in the head, expertly, just below the hairline. The died, their expressions still unchanged.

He walked past their bodies into the kitchen, and did a fast but complete search of the house, a final check that there was no one inside. He came back into the kitchen, saw a stack of paper cups by the water cooler, helped himself to a drink. There was a chair just inside the door. He sat down on it, looked out of the open door at the gyrations of the woman in the back jerking with screams and spasms in the dust of the yard. There seemed to be a lot of blood on the ground and on her clothes. It was important that she didn't bleed to death before her husband returned. His own wife had been killed in front of his eyes.

He sat and sipped the water. The woman had been screaming so loudly she was now losing her voice. Or maybe she was dying from loss of blood. The man put his cup down and knelt again and prayed on the cool tiled kitchen floor. This time his prayer was that Holby would come home soon.

2

THERE WERE TWO MEETINGS—as if the initial six-hour debate over the murders was inadequate and there had to be two. The first took place inside the Pentagon on January 20. The second, twelve days later in the Holiday Inn on Boulevard Heights, Washington. The man who briefed the four generals each time was a Major Hallam from U.S. Army Intelligence, Fort Holabird. He spoke carefully to his superiors as if he alone knew everything about the killings and was anxious they should not miss the smallest detail. The major gave the known facts at the first meeting. Twelve days later when they reassembled in a private suite in the Holiday Inn he told them about some frightening new developments.

On January 20 it was snowing in Washington. The meeting had been set for nine, but two generals commuting in from the suburbs were delayed in the traffic snarled up by the weather. The meeting started at nine-forty.

The soft-voiced major began by giving details of the latest murder. The four generals sat in silence. From the expressions on their faces they seemed somehow out of it, bemused, disoriented. Maybe it was because they had been forbidden, for security reasons, to bring their aides, and generals, as the fable goes, are naked without them. Or maybe it was that the room selected for the meeting was on the exterior wall of the Pentagon, the harsh reflection from the snow on the ground outside glaring in, confusing these men more used to office-light-artificial environments. Or maybe the brutality of these murders in suburban America of American families, husbands, wives and children, staggered even those men who just three years before had been making decisions committing thousands of lives in Vietnam.

Before the meeting Major Hallam had been told that each of the generals knew something of the story—none of them the whole of it. He decided then to begin at the beginning, and work forward. There was an exact date when the story started: the tenth of April, 1969. When the prosecutor at the court-martial summed up the events of that day he called them "the blackest hours in the history of the American Army."

Da Loc was a Vietnamese village just south of the seventeenth parallel. Army Intelligence around March, 1969, classified it as an intractable Viet Cong sympathizing village—one which would be a main supply of ordnance, food and shelter for the VC. On the tenth of April, 1969, three Chinook helicopters on a search and destroy mission landed just outside Da Loc an hour after daybreak. Eighty men of Able and Baker company, 2nd Battalion, Twenty-First Infantry, PFC's, corporals, platoon sergeants, three lieutenants, two captains and a colonel walked into the village, rounded up every inhabitant, four hundred of them, children and women as well as men, and shot them all dead at point-blank range. They then set fire to the village.

Nine months later, three lieutenants, two captains, and six of the eighty men appeared at a court-martial. The colonel who had led the raid on Da Loc had meantime been killed in a helicopter accident. For another six months and through two appeals the eyes of the world's media were on the men. The two captains, the lieutenants, and four men went to army prison for terms of from three to seven years. By 1973 most of them had been released.

In the period from November 10, 1975, to January 5, 1976, one of the captains, Joe John Gaber, and two of the ex-lieutenants, Holby and Krantz, were murdered in three different locations in America, and their wives and children butchered along with them.

The first to die had been David Krantz. He and his girlfriend, Eleanor Lammit, daughter of a Baptist minister, were found in the charred remains of a log hut in Lake Arrowhead, California. The two had been shot to death. There were no guns in the house. The police put it down to a robbery that had fouled up and turned into murder and incendiarizing.

One month later the Holby family were murdered. Military forensic experts who examined the still-smoldering remains of Holby's farmhouse near Newtown, Kansas, concluded that the murderers had waited for Holby's wife and children to return from school and for Holby himself to return from work at his local office, and then had shot the children in front of him and his wife, and then had taken his wife out into the backyard and shot her, and then finally had shot him in his living room. The house had been incendiarized with gasoline and his wife's body brought back from the garden, possibly still with some life in it, and thrown on the pyre. A burned watch dial on one of the children's wrists, with the hands still in position, showed the watch had stopped at six-thirty-four. The burned watch on Holby's wife's hand had stopped at eight minutes to seven.

The Federal Bureau of Investigation has no cross-reference system for type-grouping crimes by modus operandi. When ex-Lieutenant Henry Sickert routinely tried to get in touch with his friend Holby and heard of the fire, and then tried to get in touch with David Krantz on the other side of the country to tell him the bad news, and found Krantz and his girlfriend had died in an identical way, he thought it over, phoned a major he knew in the Pentagon and told him the curious coincidence of the deaths of these two who had been involved in the Da Loc tragedy. The Pentagon wheels turned and Army Intelligence, Fort Holabird, was alerted. Sickert was requested not to talk to press or police. Holabird put a task force of thirty men into the investigation including fifteen men to guard the remaining officers and men who'd featured in the court-martial.

A month after the massacre of the Holby family, ex-Captain Gaber of the Da Loc incident, his wife, four-year-old daughter, and two sergeants who were guarding their house near the town of Montgomery, Alabama, were all shot to death, their bodies taken inside the house, and the house burned to the ground somewhere near dawn on a Sunday morning.

Three ex-Da Loc officers, a girlfriend, families and bodyguards, had now died in different parts of America. After the butchering of the Gaber family and the two sergeants provided to protect them, the number of army operatives from Holabird assigned to the case was increased to a hundred. Half these men were put to the task of going back over every detail of the records of Vietnamese war veterans allowed into America, to try to find any who might have had connections with the village of Da Loc. Nothing was found.

The first conclusion of Army Intelligence was that at least two psychopaths had homed in on the court-martial list, and had decided to revenge the massacre of the village. The feeling was that the psychopaths would be American, probably from some freak psychotic sect. And this was the line the soft-voiced major gave to the generals at the Pentagon meeting. The debate had terminated with the generals trying to work out an approach to investigating and hunting down the murderers. They had mostly opposing ideas, but they all agreed on one point. This was an Army matter and pressure should be used to keep it such. No details should be given to the newspapers. The report in the L.A. papers had simply stated that Krantz and his girlfriend had died in a log cabin blaze. The local Newtown, Kansas, paper also ascribed the Holby deaths to some unknown accident causing a tragic fire. News of the Gaber deaths never got into the papers.

As part of their decision to keep this matter confidential, the suite in the Holiday Inn was selected for the second meeting. All Pentagon officials know that new methods of eavesdropping can be installed quickly. One answer to the problem of finding a bug-free room is to make a random choice from one of Washington's fifty good hotels and hire a suite, then immediately hold the meeting.

When the generals came back together for the February 1 meeting at the Holiday Inn most of them were by now investigating the crimes. But none of them had heard the news the soft-voiced major opened with. Across the Atlantic in Holland, technicians at the Phillips' laboratories in Eindhoven had reprocessed a faulty videotape produced by a stationary television camera hidden in the grounds of the Gaber house in Montgomery, Alabama, on the night of the murders. From the faulty videotape the technicians had clarified four pictures of a man. These had just this morning been wirephotoed from Eindhoven to the Pentagon. The wirephotos positively identified the murderer of the eleven victims as a man called Van Dhoc, a Vietnamese national, and a former captain in the victorious North Vietnamese Army.

The generals' first question was who was this Captain Van Dhoc? The second was how could a Vietnamese communist ex-captain carry out singlehandedly—if the videotape evidence was to be believed—the murders of eleven people across mainland America? Hallam had no answers. He announced that General Harris, the general commanding Fort Holabird, did have more information. He would be joining them shortly and bringing the wirephotos. Meanwhile Hallam could only offer a thumbnail biography of Van Dhoc that Holabird operatives had culled from the records of the war the nation had lost.

The Vietnamese would be about forty. Five years ago he'd been a captain in Field Operations with the NLA operating south of the DMZ. There was a captured VC photograph of part of one of their patrols, evidently of better clarity than the four wirephotos on their way from Eindhoven. The tall man in the middle of it, with a Ho Chi Minh mustache, was Dhoc.

An hour after the meeting began General Harris called to say he would be arriving in half an hour. The major who'd answered the phone relayed to the generals the chief's orders that they all go over the latest file before he arrived. This was a buff folder the major had distributed to each general at the beginning of the meeting. There were forty pages of typing. The major drew their attention to a report dealing with an item found by one of the hundred soldiers from Fort Evans who helped search the Gaber house the day after the murders. It was listed as "a bullet plaspack transparent."

General Harris, a fifty-year-old Bostonian, arrived just before noon, bringing with him the four wirephotos from the clarified videotapes. There was no question that the pictures were of the same man featured in the captured photo of the North Vietnamese patrol. The videotape had been taken from a camera hidden ten feet up a tree outside the Gaber house and showed Van Dhoc approaching the house at the start of his butchery.

"I've come to pick your brains," Harris started. "But first some coffee." And he sent the major out with the order.

"We think we've located Van Dhoc," Harris said, as soon as the major was gone, as if the Intelligence officer was suddenly someone who should not know of the discovery. "We've found him in a very logical hiding place. The clue was the plastic pack in the Gaber grounds. . . ."

At first sight the sergeant searching the grounds didn't think it was important. He'd have passed it by if his instructions hadn't been to collect everything he found. The forensic experts found that a dozen bullets had been carried in the pack—there were microscopic traces of carbide on the plastic. And on the bottom of the pack, stamped in the plastic, were the letters "RPS." It didn't take long for Holabird to find out what the code meant—"Republika Popullore e SHQIPER-ISE"—the plastic bullet pouch had been made in Albania, the only European country whose communist sympathies were with China, not Russia.

"Albania," Harris said, looking at his notes. "Anyone been there?"

The generals shook their heads.

"People's Republic of Albania, prime minister dictator Enver Hoxha." He looked at some notes he'd made. "Small country, 28,000 square kilometers, 1.9 million inhabitants, borders with Greece and Yugoslavia. A problem economy underpinned by the Chinese. About two thousand Chinese 'technicians' currently in the country."

The generals had no comment.

"What I've done is to have some data checked. Alitalia is the only western airline with scheduled flights from Trieste to Albania's capital, Tiranha. We've checked out the Alitalia passenger lists around November tenth, when Krantz and the girl died, the eighth of December, when the Holbys died, and January fifth when the Gabers died. We were looking for a name that might recur on these flight lists around the time of the murders and we found one. A 'Mr. Vandyke.' I believe is is more than a coincidence that 'Vandyke' and 'Van Dhoc' sound alike and that the arrival times before the murders and the departure flights from America were also within hours of the murders."

There was a contemplative silence for a moment, then General Patterson, special assistant to the chief of staff and a famous field general from Vietnam, spoke. "Have you solved the key question, all sixty-four thousand dollars of it? Why would Captain Van Dhoc be avenging the Da Loc massacre?"

Harris shook his head. "I don't have the full answer. There has to be one. We're going to have to find it. Obviously he must be receiving money and backup from the new government of Vietnam. And if he never gets to murder another of those court-martial names, he's already pulled off a remarkable coup. The Third World and even some of our own politicians have always said the sentences passed at the Da Loc court-martial were too light."

"Let's get this clear, Frank." General Bedale, of Army Intelligence Corps Command, addressed General Harris. "You're telling us an ex-VC commutes to America, murders a captain, two officers, their families, a girlfriend and bodyguards. Now you say he's operating from Albania. My question is how the hell are we supposed to believe all this?"

"Because they're facts, Jerome," Harris told him. "We have no alternative but to accept and act on them. This meeting is to discuss how we intend to find and kill this bastard, as quickly and quietly as possible."

3

FIFTEEN DAYS AFTER THE Holiday Inn meeting, General James Mackerras, head of U.S. Army Intelligence, Europe, walked up to the reception desk at the Hertz Rent-a-Car branch in Avenue de Friedland, Paris. The man who was waiting there, his deputy, Colonel Buckman, stood up, gave a brief salute and indicated for the general to follow him down some steps into an underground garage. Mackerras' office had ordered a Citroën 2000 CX.

An attractive Hertz blonde left a glass cubicle and came across and smiled at the general, then gave Buckman the papers and returned his Diners Club card. They got into the car. Buckman started the engine and nosed the Citroën forward up the cement ramp to join the heavy lunch-hour traffic heading down to l'Etoile.

General Mackerras didn't like Buckman. The colonel had arrived from the Pentagon full of ideas two years ago. Mackerras had listened to those ideas during several games of golf. He disliked the man's ideas as much as he hated his excellent golf. Mackerras wanted everybody to know that he saw his job as European director of Army Intelligence as mirroring the political notion of détente, maintaining the status quo. Buckman felt that U.S. Army Intelligence in Europe should be bursting with all sorts of projects and Intelligence initiatives.

Mackerras was nearing sixty, a tall blue-eyed archetype of soldier-cum-frontiersman. A brigadier general, he had come through a bloody war in Vietnam and turned from a public soldier, who had made a lot of noise and gotten the appropriate notices, into a quiet and scheming man, sitting on top of his small empire of Army European Intelligence, protecting it always from the acquisitive glances of the CIA, and waiting out his pension.

Buckman, thirty-nine, had started out to be a scholar and academic. He'd entered the Army after Korea and found, somewhat to his own surprise, a taste for Military Intelligence life. For the last two years in Europe he'd had a loose and roving brief, was in fact very much his own man, and made his way around the capitals—Bonn, Paris, London and Rome. Mackerras encouraged him to get on with his own projects, stay as far away from him as possible, and keep out of trouble—all of which Buckman did. In two years the colonel had pulled off three brilliant counterintelligence coups which were still the talk of Washington. Buckman was from New England, Mackerras from Georgia, appropriate backgrounds for a declaration of their private civil war.

Buckman prodded through the traffic, then chose the inside lane which seemed to be moving faster down Friedland, and tucked the Citroën into the traffic flow.

"How was Washington, sir?"

Mackerras, who was normally circumspect in his answers, taking his time, didn't hesitate on this occasion. "Obviously my invite was timed so I'd arrive after Holabird had already played the hands."

"What are their decisions, sir?"

This time Mackerras did not answer immediately.

Buckman had now slowed the Citroën to a halt. The traffic at the bottom of the street had snarled up. Another car drew alongside them. It was a Bentley, French license plates, chauffeur-driven, with a fat man and a beautiful girl holding hands in the back. Mackerras' eyes flicked idly from the man to the girl and back to the man as if he'd decided these two were intrinsically more deserving of his attention than the murder plot on his hands.

"Harris moved the whole operation to us, to Paris," Mackerras finally said. "The hook is that Dhoc, operating from Albania, will himself find Paris a more convenient strike. But that will be his mistake."

"Is there more than that to their reasoning?"

"At home there are now 110,000 permanent resident-refugees from Vietnam. There could be quislings among them giving aid to Dhoc in his operation. There's one other large Vietnamese community in the world, refugees from another war, the French-Indochinese War."

"Here in Paris."

"Yes, but the difference between the Paris Vietnamese community and the one back home—the French community has been static—more or less each individual known to the others—for the last twenty years, since France pulled its ass out of 'Nam. A strange face like Dhoc's turning up in the Paris Vietnamese community would be noticed. Especially as we're now going to set up alerting the community."

"But there would have to be a reason why Dhoc would come to Paris."

Mackerras was quiet for a moment. He seemed to be looking around the car, studying it. It was a new car, less than three hundred kilometers on the odometer. He was becoming an expert on hired cars—they had become his main source of transport since two years before, when listening devices of unknown origin had been found on all the vehicles in the senior car pool at SHAPE Headquarters, Versailles.

"You got half the Washington news," Mackerras said at last. "Tell me, who do you think were the key men in the Da Loc court-martial?"

Buckman looked puzzled, like he expected a catch in the question. "The two officers."

"Names?"

"One was Holby—another Cantwell."

"Caswell," Mackerras corrected.

Buckman nodded. The traffic had started forward

again and he was heading the car into the gyrations of traffic around Place de l'Etoile.

"We know what happened to Holby. That leaves ex-Lieutenant Stephen Caswell. Holabird convinced him. He arrives in Paris tomorrow. We have to set up a 'T' program for him. That's yours."

Buckman said nothing, still working out the implications of the general's words. He moved the Citroën neatly into the traffic converging from the right, concentrated now to cut through the cars and blaring horns to line up again for the left exit for the route south to Porte d'Auteuil.

"Van Dhoc operates out of Albania . . ." Buckman was thinking it over. "Key name of the Da Loc court-martial is brought to Paris and exposed. The idea is to isolate Van Dhoc in Paris and grab him when he arrives and goes for Caswell. I wonder if there's one element missing in General Harris' plan, sir."

"You've decided there is one, Buckman?"

"The general may be underestimating Van Dhoc's intelligence."

"No one's underestimating his intelligence. The question is, how mad is he? How crazy? . . ."

The colonel said nothing, but his expression was clearly dissatisfied.

Mackerras was studying the traffic again. "We parade Caswell around and set up a trap when Van Dhoc makes his move. That's the front plan. Now here's the backup. Failing Dhoc's appearance here we are to organize a mission into Albania, find the fucker, and cut him down."

4

THIRTEEN DAYS AFTER MACKERRAS' return from Washington, a man in a gray Burberry coat sat in the back of an Army Chevrolet in the stalled traffic outside l'Assemblée nationale. He was an American in his midforties, his face pale and eyes shadowed with travel. He had arrived at Orly a half-hour ago, the single passenger on a U.S. military transport that had flown him across the Atlantic direct from Hector Field, Fargo, North Dakota. The flight had been a rough one and the transport plane ill ventilated. Paris was cold this morning, and the skies shed a soft rain, but he had both rear windows of the car rolled down.

His eyes studied the fortress façade of the Assemblée, uniformed police, guns held ready, on their shifty-eyed patrols. No change there. He stared out across the dull gray river to the Right Bank skyline, no major transformations. Paris had been less raped by the office building entrepreneurs than most cities. In fact on the drive in from the airport he'd been surprised that the suburbs and the city had looked almost identical to the Paris of twenty-three years ago when he'd last been here, on his honeymoon.

The man in the Burberry pondered his memories. He had been all Army in those days, setting off on the ambitious route of a career soldier in a hurry and angry that a mistaken pregnancy, later followed by a miscarriage, had produced an unwanted wife who might slow him down. He had walked a lot and alone in Paris during that honeymoon. He used to stroll from a little hotel in the rue des Beaux Arts along to the Assemblée each morning while she slept off her drinking of the previous night. Nineteen fifty-three had been an interesting time in France's history. Three hundred miles to the east, Iron Curtain diplomacy was already causing France problems in its cherished colonial possessions. Full-scale war was raging in the northern states of Vietnam, with red guerrillas openly confronting the Emperor Bao Dai. But it had never occurred to him as he'd read those stories in the *Paris Tribune* that one day France would step aside in Vietnam and turn that country into a private hell for him, and the graveyard for American foreign policy.

The dark-khaki Chevrolet drove up the riverbank toward Pont Neuf, crossed at the Pont des Arts, its destination a tall building in rue Bailleul behind the Palais du Louvre. There was a brass plaque set in a wall to the left of the front door of the building. The legend on the sign read "Club Militaire de France, Privé." The door of the club was closed and shuttered. The driver of the Chevrolet, a sergeant of the Twenty-First Armored Group, got out of the car, unrolled an umbrella and opened the rear door. The American stepped out, took the umbrella and looked toward the shuttered door of the building.

As if his look had triggered some mechanism, the door opened behind the shutter. An old man in blue dungarees tackled the locks and swung them away. The man followed his sergeant driver but didn't offer him the cover of the umbrella. They walked up the front steps and into a marbled hall. It was about thirty feet long, twenty high, and had a dozen doors off it. The man in the dungarees had gone, presumably to alert a reception party.

"You want I wait, sir?" the sergeant chauffeur asked. The man nodded. He had no instructions on what to expect. He turned and caught sight of himself in a large faded glass mirror behind a low antique Provençal cupboard by the front door. The mirror showed his tiredness, the strain in the blue eyes behind the steel-rimmed glasses. He wore a Brooks Brothers suit. He didn't look like a soldier, more a banker, with the furrows on his forehead the result of concentration on figures rather than the problems met by a man who'd run a Special Forces Camp in Vietnam. Three years ago, aged forty-two, he had been a colonel. At that age with any sort of record and those knowing eyes he should have made general. And he would have but for a single mistake which had sent him out of the Army two years ago.

Then three days ago a messenger had come to him in his retirement, living at his brother's farm. The man had been dispatched by the Pentagon to tell him that he would be given a second chance. But no explanations. Then there had been a briefing in Washington. He was told about the job, but not too many details, and mostly not the important ones. Well maybe he was going to learn them now.

A door opened halfway down the hall on the right. A colonel in spit-and-polish uniform stepped out, and gave him and the chauffeur a once-over. Then he moved quietly down the marble tiles toward him. "Buckman," he said, and delivered a soft handshake.

"John Leeming," the tall man said back.

"Good flight?" Buckman inquired in his New England accent.

"Weather held us up at Gander, four hours," said Leeming. The colonel would know that, but Leeming felt that a few words would ease the way.

"Tell me, you want to start work? Or check out your hotel, get some shut-eye?"

"I'm ready for work," Leeming said, wondering again, as he'd wondered many times in the past three days, what exactly the work would entail.

"Follow me." Buckman was already moving up the hall, feet echoing on the marble. Leeming turned to the driver. "Wait." Then he strode off after the retreating figure.

At the end of the hall Buckman opened a door to a small low-roofed corridor.

"You're going to meet someone in a swimming pool. He'll ask you questions. You may talk to him quite openly, though he doesn't want you to see who he is."

They had reached the door at the end of the corridor. Buckman opened the door. Leeming stepped through and heard it immediately close behind him. It was almost pitch dark, some drift of half-light filtered down through cracks in the frames of the blackout glass above the pool, enough at least to see the four walls and the tile surrounding the sixty-foot-long swimming pool. A figure was out there floating on its back, hardly causing a stir in the gently lapping water. The features were indistinguishable, except for the gleam of the bald head.

Leeming thought he would wait for the swimmer to speak. The man must be aware of his presence but all Leeming heard were deep breaths, held, and expelled, in a rush, and for a moment he wondered if the floating figure was in some trouble. Then Leeming realized the man was doing breathing exercises, or maybe water therapy. Finally the deep breathing stopped, and the voice started, low and American.

"Welcome to Paris, Colonel Leeming. I won't identify myself except to say I carry as much authority as anyone you'll meet. Now tell me what you've been briefed on this venture."

Leeming's eyes tried to pierce the gloom. Some current in the swimming pool, maybe the filter pumps, was gently swinging the man around in a lazy axis. He wondered why he wouldn't identify himself, what weight of authority he had, who he worked for? If he was Army Intelligence he'd have no real reason not to introduce himself. What then—did he belong to the CIA or some other clandestine operation? From Leeming's own experience in dealing with Service Intelligence organizations he knew that it would be impossible to mount a major initiative like the Van Dhoc hunt without certain Pentagon groups sniffing it out and turning up to see if there was a bite of the bone for them. The current had swung the man around now, so that Leeming was addressing the back of his head.

"I'm to train a subject to carry out an assassination."

"Nothing else?"

"Nothing."

"You have to examine ex-Lieutenant Caswell, the Caswell of the Da Loc incident, and tell us, prove to us, whether he is or is not capable of this mission. And if you think he is, you'll train him to do the task." The floating man's indecipherable face swung into view again.

"May I know what kind of assassination? Is it a major figure?"

"You'll evaluate this man exactly as you selected and trained men in your Special Forces Camp in 'Nam. Understood?"

"Yes, sir."

"General Mackerras will tell you everything you need to know. I, as an anonymous person, have to say something to you that the general would not be permitted to say. Are you listening carefully?"

"Yes, sir."

"At the end of this enterprise only five men in the world—my official figure—will have the knowledge of what took place. My unofficial figure is four. Realistically I don't believe Caswell will come back. I must make clear to you the security of this project and our continued discretion when the news breaks in the press. Both of these elements are as important as the carrying out of the task. Can you appreciate that this is possible?"

Leeming said it gently. "Yes."

"Good," the voice said. "Now we have some equipment critical to the op's success. An old gun, a Siamese Mauser rebarreled to Russian 7.62 bore. A small plane called the Feiseler Storch. Have you ever flown in a Feiseler Storch, Colonel?"

"No," Leeming said.

"Go and try it."

The interview was over. The bald-headed man was

swimming slowly away to the far side of the pool. He found the pool steps, climbed clear of the water and turned in the colonel's direction. "The Feiseler's an old plane. Axis. World War Two. We have a pilot who says he can do certain things with it. If he can, the project's feasible. If he can't, take out life insurance. Yes?"

Leeming couldn't decide whether the remark was meant to be humorous or practical.

5

THE AFF AIRPORT AT Neuilly is ten miles from Orly. It was two P.M., five hours from the time the Army plane bearing its sole passenger had arrived from America. Buckman had the necessary passes to get through the outer- and inner-gate sentries, and he seemed to know where he was going. He pointed the way to his driver. They moved along the inner perimeter road past low hangars, most of them containing Mystère fighters being serviced. After a kilometer they came to a halt by a small double hangar. Outside this there was an English Triumph TR6 sports car parked, with a large man sitting in it. The rain, which had cloaked Paris all morning, had in the last half-hour started to develop into a storm.

The man got out of the sports car and headed toward them. The driver had parked the Army Chevrolet to one side of the hangar's apron to allow room for the plane inside to be taxied out.

Leeming's eyes went from the man coming toward them through the rain to the plane sitting in the hangar. It was a single-engine, high-wing monoplane in brown, green and gray camouflage. A four-seater, unarmed, he thought, until he caught sight of the barrel of a machine gun sticking out of the cabin roof. The plane had high ground clearance, long spindle legs with unspatted wheels and a complex arrangement of ailerons with large spoilers along the front edge of the wing. The whole contraption gave the impression of having been put together from the spare parts of a dozen small aircraft, which was possibly the case. It had obviously been designed for a purpose other than for traveling through the air with optimum aerodynamics.

Buckman got out of the car and went to intercept the man. They had a brief exchange of words—Leeming couldn't hear what was said—and then they were walking back to the Chevrolet. Buckman opened the rear door and the big man got in beside Leeming.

"Major Meyer, USAF. Colonel Leeming," said Buckman. Leeming gave a nod.

The Air Force major fixed his eyes on Leeming for five seconds as if sizing him up, and then turned and spoke to Buckman.

"Are we going acrobatic in this shit?"

Buckman looked out through the arcing windshield wipers at the soaking airfield. He nodded. Then he said to no one in particular, "The Feiseler comes with a French pilot."

Meyer shrugged. "I've known some of these AFF spec pilots. They're crazy. We're crazy to test fly in this gale with one of them." Then he looked at Leeming. "You coming up?"

Buckman answered for him. "We all go. The crate has to produce its performance four up, or the deal is off."

"If the French spec kills us, we should have someone on the ground to write home."

"The general's orders are we all get to fly." Buckman pulled out an envelope and handed it to Meyer. "The rest of his orders."

Meyer took the manila envelope, pulled out a single sheet of paper, and read it.

"Fuck," he said softly.

Buckman looked sharply at Meyer, as if annoyed at his language.

"He wants us to land this abortion in eighty feet." Meyer was looking at the tiny plane through the rain.

He asked the question as if he was thinking to himself. "Why eighty feet?"

"I once saw a plane land on a bridge a hundred and fifty feet long," Leeming offered.

"A bridge," Meyer said, like he was musing on it.

"The plane I saw landing on a bridge a hundred and fifty feet long didn't make it," Leeming added.

There was a silence for a moment and then Buckman asked Meyer if he'd ever heard of a Feiseler before.

"Sure. But never flown one. Kraut. This one manufactured in '44, makes it over thirty years old. General M's office sent me the C of A report. It's okay. Storch specializes in short take-offs and landings. Beginning of the war it was built in Germany, then construction moved to the slave factories in Puteaux, France. Many variants. This is the F11 56C-1 staff transport. Fourseater 7.9mm MG 15 rear cabin, speed 110 knots, range 250 plus, enough apparently to get to our target, assuming somebody tells me what the target is. Buckman?"

Buckman shrugged off the question. Obviously a major of the USAF was not to be included in the confidence of a high level Army Intelligence initiative, and should know it.

"You tell me why *you'd* use a thirty-year-old box kite?" Buckman asked.

"If the mission's behind the Ironworks," Meyer answered.

Leeming realized it had been years since he'd heard the term "Ironworks"—the Military Intelligence word for countries behind the Iron Curtain. Forces Intelligence vocabulary was so different from CIA language which always sounded as if it had been invented by a Madison Avenue agency specializing in half-truths. People were not killed in CIA language, they were "wasted." An enemy politician was not assassinated, his life was "terminated with extreme ferocity." The CIA would have some elaborate term for countries behind the Iron Cur-

tain. It was good to hear the old graphic Forces term
"Ironworks."

"Why a Storch?" Buckman repeated.

"Anyone can fly under radar. They have a new trick,
a heat scan net—picks up the heat radiations from a jet
engine. The Storch engine will be heat-insulated. You
can fly it under radar to Moscow, land it in Red
Square—and that's the first time the Rusks would
know."

Buckman was studying the Storch, calculating. "I've
never heard of a plane that could land in eighty feet."

"Here comes the man who'll prove you're right,"
Meyer said.

A battered newish Peugeot 504 came fast down the
perimeter road. It braked by the Chevrolet and a small
thin man, neat in the uniform of a captain in the French
Air Arm, stepped out, saluted, put up an umbrella and
pointed to the Feiseler to indicate he would meet the
group inside the hangar.

Meyer, Buckman and Leeming got out of the car and
jogged through the rain for the shelter of the hangar.

"De Laubenque," the French pilot introduced himself.

Meyer made the other introductions. Then he relayed
the general's orders to the French pilot. Eighty feet was
translated into meters as Buckman and de Laubenque
debated whether the Feiseler could land in that distance. The Frenchman had some difficulty speaking
English but less problems understanding it. "The Storch
with four of us loaded, will land in twenty-five meters. I
imagine. Just about."

"You seem pretty confident of that. How can you be
sure?" Meyer asked.

"Have you flown this plane?" the Frenchman demanded.

"No."

"Then how can you have knowledge of its landing
performance?"

"I see this lousy weather ceiling. I know how long twenty-five meters is."

The Frenchman was getting angry, as if he had a personal stake in the plane's performance. "I will show you." He picked up an empty twenty-liter oil drum inside the hangar, put up his umbrella and walked out into the rain, turning immediately right at the hangar doors. The three watched him stride out twenty-five paces starting from the inside wall of the hangar. He put the drum down on the grass. He returned and informed them, "I fly, touch down by the drum. I stop the plane before I hit the wall. You say it will not stop—it takes longer than twenty-five meters? If you are right, I hit the wall. I say I will stop in time." He turned and headed for the right entry door to the Feiseler.

As if he felt that a lengthy and pointless debate was about to start, Meyer turned to the other two and said softly, "Let's fly."

One after another they entered the cramped cabin of the Feiseler. It took a couple of minutes to squeeze their way into the metal bucket seats and strap in. Then de Laubenque pressed the servo which turned over the V8 engine, the prop cranked twice and the engine shuddered to life. Leeming looked from Meyer to the French pilot, both were concentrating on the sound and feel of the machine as the engine warmed quickly up to four-and-a-half thousand—the sound jack-hammering through the cockpit. Leeming had almost forgotten that most startling characteristic of all old war planes— cabin noise. To communicate now he would have to shout.

The French pilot throttled full power. The engine sang up from 3,500 to 6,000 in a back-thumping surge, and the plane was hurling itself forward on its small wheels across the uneven grass, and they were airborne, as if some unseen force had pulled the plane up into the sky.

Through the narrow observation bridge of glass running along the bottom of the Storch side windows,

Leeming studied the familiar landmarks of Paris, Eiffel and Notre Dame, he could tick them off just below the horizon, almost screened from view by the rain scratching along the windows. Paris, a beautiful city to so many—but Leeming had always found it full of cold hollows, ever since that first unhappy introduction. But he was not going to dwell on that now. He was wondering about the Feiseler pilot and the brick wall at the end of his boast.

He was hunched in the rear seat behind the large body of Meyer, himself shoulder-to-shoulder with de Laubenque. Buckman's shoulder was pressed against Leeming's. Buckman must also have been thinking about de Laubenque's boast. He tapped Meyer on the back and shouted, "How's the weather alter landing characteristics?"

Meyer paused for a moment. The French pilot with one final ease on the throttle lifted the Feiseler up to a cruising ceiling at ten thousand feet.

"We're hitting grass. No Maxeret antiskid. This box will slide, unless de Laubenque pulls a stall drop."

"What's that?"

"If you have doubts, tell the man."

Buckman was now obviously considering the real implications of landing for the first time. He tapped the Frenchman's shoulder. "Mister." His voice was loud and hard. "We got ourselves into some competition. Why not land in soft grass? We'll measure wheel tracks to check whether they're under twenty-five meters."

The French pilot's answer was to push the joystick straight forward. The Storch stood on end. Leeming found himself thrown hard into his seat harness. He heard an oath from his own lips.

The plane was falling, spiraling down the sky. The French pilot arced forward on his harness, like the others, judging the altitude now by sight, not by altimeter, which in a plane being driven almost vertically into the ground at three hundred knots loses micro-second accuracy. Leeming, frozen immobile, pinned by his harness, saw dimly through the rain the gray fields of wet grass and camouflaged hangars coming up to annihilate them, saw the tiny hangar, almost tried to place it geographically for a last compass fix before they hit it—and the Chevrolet, and its driver—and had the life crushed out of all of them. Then suddenly the Storch was out of the slide and the joystick was falling back easily in de Laubenque's hand, and the landing wheels hit grass, and Leeming saw three things. The oil drum that the French pilot had placed on the grass, the horrified face of the Army chauffeur, and the brick wall of the side of the hangar. He felt the wheels bite and miss, and skid, and saw de Laubenque throw the rudder over, and the right wing dipped and sliced into the grass and mud. As Leeming saw sky he braced himself for the impact that was to come—and it didn't. The right wing dug in again and the plane spun lazily twice, the second spin lifting it a dozen feet off the ground. And they stopped five feet from the solid wall, the side of the plane to it. De Laubenque cut the engine. There was silence in the Feiseler.

Meyer coughed to clear his throat, as if about to make an angry pronouncement. But when the words came they were soft voiced. "Wasn't exactly a direct approach. Can we do it again, Captain de Laubenque? But this time we have to touch down straightline."

"You'll excuse us," Buckman said. His voice appeared calm. "I got to take Leeming to the general." He squeezed up out of his seat, unlocked the exit hatch and cranked himself out of the plane.

Leeming nodded to the other two and followed Buckman out. He would think about the incident later. He would recall that Buckman and Meyer, in the little plane heading across the grass at a hundred miles an hour, apparently unavoidably to hit the brick wall of the hangar, had said nothing, no oaths from their mouths like the one which had come involuntarily from his. It was important for him to realize the quality of the men he was teamed with on this project, the details of which he hoped the general would now reveal.

It also occurred to him as he followed Buckman across the grass to the Chevrolet that the whole thing might just have been an elaborately staged setup to test his own courage.

6

THE THREE-ACRE SPRAWL of the offices of SHAPE Headquarters, Versailles, built in the fifties to house key personnel of European Allied defense, had not worn the years well. Leeming saw office blocks with blistered paint, steel huts with rusting roofs, and torn wire fencing badly patched. The buildings may have decayed but the activity around them had not diminished. In the fifties the Allies had joined their European forces under a Central Command structure to deal with the threat from the east. Twenty years later the threat was not only still present, but stronger than ever.

Leeming studied the buildings looking gray and somber under the rain clouds still low-screening the horizon. The sheets of rain had gone but had left a persistent drizzle hazing the Chevrolet's windshield wipers. He was in the back of the car, Buckman in front with the driver. They went straight past the building with its ten-foot sign in French, English and German. "Reception— All Visitors report." The Chevrolet moved into a cement maze, down long avenues of prefabricated office blocks.

The general's office was a small building with a Cadillac Seville parked outside. On the Cadillac's rear fender was a black rank insignia with two gold metal stars set diagonally. The driver of the Chevrolet braked and tucked the car into a gap between the Caddy and a row of privet.

Leeming followed Buckman across to the building. A

33

Marine sentry was posted just inside the door. Buckman waited as Leeming showed his Army warrant. The marine took his time, studying the warrant, its picture, Leeming, and the SHAPE Security Clear. Then he nodded. They took the stairs from the lobby to the second floor. Leeming noted that there were no windows at all in the lobby or up the staircase that led to the general's suite.

A secretary in an outer office stood up as soon as they walked in, and without a word disappeared into the general's office. A moment later she was out and beckoning to Buckman. Buckman went in and closed the door. Leeming sat down on a hard chair by a low table and picked up the morning edition of the *International Herald Tribune*. The door to the general's office opened and Buckman came out, the remains of a scowl on his face.

"I have to deliver something to you at your hotel. You'll go back there after the general?"

He nodded.

Buckman indicated for Leeming to go into the office. Leeming walked past him into the room. The general was on the phone delivering monosyllables. He gave a vague nod to Leeming's salute and pointed to a leather chair in front of his desk. Leeming sat. The general offered instructions into the phone, then dropped the receiver back on its cradle and looked at Leeming.

"I studied your record carefully." Mackerras' words sounded like they were already edged with criticism. "You were a white hope, until '69. Then you're in 'Nam and instead of getting your first star, you end up ten miles from the front line, doing what? Running a Special Forces camp. Fools' cul-de-sac in any Army career. Then the incident happened. I read the transcript of your court-martial. With all the ambivalence of 'Nam morality floating around, how come you didn't slice off a piece and put up a real fight?"

Leeming allowed a moment of silence, some form of mute comment about his desire not to pursue the subject.

"There was nothing ambivalent about the facts, General, just the interpretation."

"Your wife died in '67?"

"Yes, sir."

"Did that hit bad?"

The question stopped him for a few seconds. It was a rare occasion now when people asked about the death of his wife. She had died in an auto accident—a collision with a truck. She'd been drunk, and skidded her car under a truck's tailgate. When it happened he'd been alone on Army leave in Hawaii. He didn't even have to identify her body—his brother had done that. She'd died on an Easter weekend. He hadn't been able to get a plane seat home for two days and almost missed the funeral. "To be truthful, no, sir, we were technically separated."

"Why did you take on an SFC?"

"I was confused in 'Nam at the time. Ambivalence wasn't confined to morality."

"It was no time for any serving officer to be confused."

Leeming nodded. He'd heard that answer before.

"You should have quit the Army, Leeming."

"Yes, sir."

"Instead of waiting for a court-martial to do it for you." Mackerras still looked as if he had not made up his mind. "The résumé of the court proceedings says how, it doesn't say why. D'you have a brief answer as to why you took the extraordinary step of ordering four hundred men to retreat in the face of the enemy?"

"The orders I gave to my SFC command was a tactical forty-eight-hour withdrawal pending a weather clear."

"That's one definition of retreat. Go on."

"It was one of the first occasions in the war when the VC used armor. I received intelligence that a division of the enemy were to attack our positions with armor. Our camp had no armor. I called up for air strikes but the weather had fouled up. And everything, including possible Huey FS support, was grounded. I didn't want to see four hundred men cut down by tank ordnance. I pulled them out."

"SFC's were supposed to take the initiative of strike and hold into VC territory."

"Against armor?"

"High Command didn't agree with you."

"That is correct, sir."

Mackerras lapsed into silence studying the man. "On the records you're still guilty as charged. If you accomplish your part in this mission successfully, High Command will reconvene the court-martial, and a relook at your case will be made to favor an acquittal."

Leeming nodded. It was basically the deal that had been explained in Washington.

"You say your wife's dead," Mackerras said quietly. "What's left? Family?"

"Brother."

"Ex-enlisted man?"

"Army."

"What does he do for a living?"

"Farmer."

"Good," Mackerras said.

Leeming knew why he said it. If he went missing, the Pentagon would turn up on brother George's doorstep to ask for his silence, and they would be talking to an ex-Army man, not to a lawyer or radical.

"When do I get a full briefing, sir?"

The general shrugged as if somehow the question was irrelevant. "You accompany Caswell around Paris. At the same time you train him for a hit in Albania." The general picked up a file and lobbed it across the desk. Leeming caught it and opened it. There were a few copies of Pentagon and Fort Holabird intelligence memos, and half a dozen photographs of Van Dhoc.

"That is the sum of information you may have at the moment. There's a Control Hold on further information and the go-ahead on the Albanian initiative."

"How do I train a man to tasks that are not specifically delineated, sir?"

"You do it. He has to shoot a Siamese Mauser, sit in

a Feiseler Storch, para-drop, shoot. Then walk a
hundred miles through some mountain ranges home.
That's it. You have two weeks."

"If he's not the right material?"

"Your job is assessing his capabilities."

"When do I meet him?"

"Seven-thirty this evening."

Leeming stood up. The interview seemed to be over.

"One final element. We in Army Intelligence have a
few problems of our own at the moment. The pressure
is on us since the disbanding of our field operations at
the end of 'Nam, for us, and Naval and Air Force
Intelligence, to clear out of all areas not precisely ac-
tioned by field activities, like ONI's foreign Naval
Intelligence and Air Force's International Liaison Division. None of this you quote me on. The Service Intelligence departments are losing out to the CIA. If we pull
off this job it may prove a blow to the aspirations of the
Central Intelligence Agency who wish officially or unofficially to take us over. This operation is vital to us."
There was a pause. "Do you understand this? D'you understand what I'm saying?"

"Yes, sir," Leeming said.

Mackerras got up, turned to the window and looked
out into the rain. "Nice to have you working with us.
Buckman left his car to take you to your hotel. Keep in
touch."

"Yes, sir," Leeming said, saluted, and walked out.

7

THE FORMER LIEUTENANT ACCUSED in the Da Loc court-martial and the only officer to serve a full four years in an Army prison raised his earmuffs, squinted through the telescopic sight on the Mauser, and fired off six shots in rapid succession. Leeming looked through binoculars at the paper target positioned on its strings fifty feet away. Caswell's shots had cut the center out of it.

They were on a *baigneuse* floating on the Seine moored just down the river from Pont Solferino. The huge converted Seine barge had undergone two recent transformations. First it had been a floating swimming pool, with two stories of superstructure including a nightclub. That operation had gone bankrupt. Now "The Rifle Club of Paris," a semiofficial government-backed organization, had taken it over and reconverted it into an indoor rifle range.

Buckman had telephoned Leeming at the George V and told him to rendezvous at the barge. When Leeming arrived Buckman was in the tiny foyer just off the main gangplank with Caswell and an official of the Rifle Club. Buckman had handed a rifle in a webbing case to Leeming and asked him to sign for it. Leeming felt this a curious formality for a gun that was going to be used in an assassination, but had said nothing and signed. Buckman had then turned to the official whom he hadn't introduced and asked the man to conduct the

two down to the range. Then he'd made his excuses
about another appointment and gone off.

Leeming and Caswell had followed the official down
into the neon-lighted steel insides of the hull. There
were a dozen people among the twenty stands on the
range, some in Naval and Army uniforms, most of them
firing small arms. The official handed them earmuffs.
Leeming checked the Mauser over thoroughly. It was
an old gun, very carefully reconditioned. He tested the
firing mechanism, then the barrel rebore. Then he took
out a case of shells and handed the gun and shells wordlessly to Caswell.

Within the first dozen shots Leeming knew that Caswell was a considerable marksman. Leeming put down
his binoculars. "Nice group. You're competitive standard?"

"Colonel, if I wasn't two months ago, I've been practicing since my friends got killed."

Leeming studied Caswell as he reloaded. Buckman,
on his car ride, had been right in the description he'd
given. This twenty-eight-year-old veteran, who in the
last years had lived through several hells, Vietnam, Da
Loc, the court-martial, prison, had none of that experience etched anywhere on his face. Buckman had said he
looked more like a boy than a man. He did. A mop of
blond hair, recently trimmed but untidy on top, a sham-
bling gait, an easy smile, perfectly disguised with youth
and inexperience the person within the mask, and made
the living contradiction to the man's history and record.

Here was a man whose picture had appeared, with
the others accused, a thousand times on the front page
of every American newspaper over the period of the
court hearings and appeals. They had all been carefully
groomed for those appearances—and maybe for the
years beyond. Caswell seemed awkward, affable, a
blameless adolescent rather than a mature killer. The
disguise was perfect. Leeming pondered whether the
man in fact had started to live the disguise—to dwell
behind the walls between himself and the nightmare of

Da Loc. Leeming knew that it was no part of his job to philosophize on the past—his or Caswell's.

"Where I come from, Winnetka, Illinois, we paddle our boat on Lake Michigan and think about the day the Chicago ghettos are going to start the Revolution eighteen miles downwater. I go twice a week to the Winnetka Rifle Club with other 'Nam vets. Chicago may be the place where that revolution is going to initiate, Colonel. It'll be me and my friends who'll just have to go down there and stop it."

Leeming didn't feel he had to comment on the observation. "How does the gun pull?"

"Right. Few millimeters. Very small."

"Can you correct?"

Caswell put on his muffs again, and sighted along the rifle. It was fitted with a heavy 4X Russian scope with micro-adjustment. He pulled off four shots. The first three in quick succession. Then he made an adjustment to the scope, and fired again.

"That's fine-adjusted."

The Siamese Mauser that Caswell was firing was a well-used gun, maybe forty years old, but steel and stock shining. Buckman had told Leeming the gun had been rebarreled for Russian 7.62mm bullets, the sort of cartridges that would be in the possession of any Albanian farmer or hunter. He'd also told him that the Russian-cased bullets were trimmed to 1.980 inches, filled with H-335 powder giving a velocity of 3092, a medium but accurate punch at thirty meters. These were details that Leeming had asked for, and Buckman already had at his fingertips. Leeming had wondered why an old gun had been specified. An obvious explanation—the hope that using a standard but slightly out of date, easily identifiable bullet like the 7.62mm, might confuse any pursuers into thinking the assassin was an Albanian citizen and not someone from outside the country. Leeming didn't think this an adequate enough reason. The other possibility for using this ordnance was that the gun was going to shoot something other than a bullet, something with a sharper entry giving a higher velocity and accuracy, but he realized that to speculate about that would be a waste of time.

"Again." Leeming spilled out more bullets. Caswell reloaded, started hammering a new target with the same great speed and pinpoint accuracy.

Then Leeming noticed the interest of the other shooters. Besides the small arms there was some high-class artillery around, like Hollands, and Pedersens, and Franchis. The club men were beginning to spot the results that Caswell was getting from the vintage Mauser.

"We're becoming conspicuous," Leeming said gently to Caswell.

"Isn't that the brief?"

"We'll come back tomorrow."

"I'm getting to see you tomorrow, Colonel?"

"Mr. Caswell, as of now, we spend twenty-four hours a day in each other's company."

"That right, Colonel?"

"That's right."

"Okay, but not tonight. I got this girlfriend."

"Girlfriend? How long have you been in Paris? Six days? How come you got a girlfriend?"

"How in hell in Paris after six days would I not have a girl?"

Leeming debated. Maybe he could have a last night free—training on the rifle range could be cut out because of the excellence of his shooting.

"Colonel, what plans you got for dinner tonight?"

"I just rode the Atlantic with a lot of delay on the flight. I'll get some sleep . . ."

"You got to eat. Be my guest and meet my girl."

He hesitated to turn him down. It was Day One of his job. It was important to spend time with Caswell if, as Mackerras had told him, his main task would be assessing his personality as well as his aptitudes.

"Colonel, I need one more night with my girl." Caswell was speaking gently. "I'll tell you why. I don't think a lot of this project. This could be my last night with her—or any other broad."

They took a cab to rue de Duras off Faubourg St. Honoré.

"His name is Franjou. He's four and a half feet high. He manufactures all the sugar in France," Caswell said.

"What are you talking about?"

"Franjou. Rich. He keeps her," Caswell said slowly, as if he thought Leeming was not concentrating. "They've been together a long time. He found her four years ago in the nightclubs in Faubourg. You know, a *chanteuse?* She had a good voice, but no good with all that went with it."

"How did you meet her?" Leeming asked.

"First day in Paris, I leave the hotel to go to a liquor store off the Champs-Elysées. I walk in the store, pick up some Scotch. This beautiful creature is in front of me near the cashier, taking down some gin from a shelf. By accident she knocks over three bottles and they smash on the floor. The proprietor goes mad, screaming and gesticulating." Caswell simulated the waving of arms. "He's demanding she pays for the booze. I step in, threaten the guy, get her out."

He stopped talking, thinking back over the space of six days, a puzzled expression on his face. "It's hard to explain to you—as hard for me to understand—but in just a few days she's come to mean a lot to me. It's crazy. She had so much class she makes everyone I've ever been involved with look like a whore. Yet she's a hooker. It's lousy—I make the first real relationship in my life and you guys are sending me out to face a psycho who's killed everything he's ever aimed at."

"He won't get you."

"I'm glad you think so, Colonel, because I don't." Caswell gave a sudden little shrug as if his own opinion didn't matter. "Her name's Lara. She's not French, she's originally from Poland. She's got all that Polish emotion. If she feels something, she really tells you. . . ."

The apartment building in rue de Duras had a court-yard behind heavy wooden gates. Caswell instructed the taxi to drive in. He got out, paid the cab, led Leeming up the stone steps to the front door of the main apartment, and pressed the bell.

The white-painted doors opened and an English butler stood there, no welcome in his eyes for Caswell.

"Good evening, Monsieur."

"Mademoiselle Lara?"

The butler stood aside for the two men to enter. Behind the doors was a narrow hallway with antique mirrors reflecting themselves. The two men gave the butler their coats and followed him into a small drawing room.

The first thing that struck Leeming, almost surprised him, was her exceptional looks. Somehow it hadn't occurred to him that Caswell's pickup in a liquor store would turn out to be so beautiful. Caswell introduced him. "Lara, this is Mr. John Leeming."

"Come in." The voice was low and there was another accent underlying the French. She dismissed the butler with a nod and gestured Leeming to a chair. "Stephen has told me a lot about you."

Her blond hair was polished to the quality of porcelain, the same paleness to her skin—and no makeup. She was dressed in a dark green blazer suit with long skirt, which looked simple enough but had probably cost a fortune, and which didn't disguise the litheness and suppleness of her body. She was about five-foot-nine but did not seem tall.

He estimated her age at around thirty-five to thirty-eight, which made her ten years older than Caswell. Although she might be flattered by the attentions of a man ten years her junior, Leeming knew she'd have no trouble gaining the attention of any man.

"Tell me if you've made plans for tonight?" She had turned to Caswell.

"Sure. I'm taking us all out to dinner. Then we'll go on and break up some bars . . . Unless you've a better idea."

"Offer John Leeming a drink," she told him.

"Scotch on the rocks," Leeming said to Caswell's look.

Caswell made his way over to an escritoire which

contained a bar. "The usual?" he asked Lara. She nodded.

Leeming's eyes went around the expensive apartment
trying to reconcile the idea of Caswell and this sophisticated woman in these surroundings.

"I understand you're quite an old friend of Stephen's?" she said.

Caswell answered for him. "Many years. We were in
'Nam together. We used to shoot gooks and dice, burn a
few hooches, share a few girls."

Leeming presumed she didn't know about the lieutenant and Da Loc, wondered what that knowledge
would do to her feelings and wondered if it was possible
to separate the two—Caswell at Da Loc, from Caswell
in Paris. Maybe it was possible.

"Share?" she questioned.

"Always," Caswell said. "Girls are for sharing."

Leeming took this news without comment. Lara's
eyes turned on him a little warily. "You really shared
girls with Stephen?"

Leeming shrugged and turned slightly to focus on Caswell's idiot performance at the bar. He was starting to
pour jiggers from various liquor bottles into a cocktail
shaker with overly dramatic gestures, as if he was the
world's greatest cocktail maker. Leeming suddenly felt
sorry for him.

"But first we have to get him in the mood," Caswell
said and poured the drink into a glass, handed it to her,
then stood back like an alchemist who'd just got the for-
mula right. "Taste that and tell me if it's right."

She tasted, nodded, indicated for him to sit down
next to her on a settee.

"We've never shared a girl. That must be his idea of
a joke," Leeming said quietly.

"He exaggerates about everything." She sounded as if
she was disappointed to hear the two men did not share
girls.

"Not about you," Leeming said.

She seemed perplexed by his remark. "What did he
say about me?"

"He said you were beautiful."

She looked Leeming straight in the eyes and then took a sip of the cocktail. "I'm surprised he found time to talk of me. His favorite subject, his obsession, is you."

"Hey Lara, you make that sound dirty." Caswell laughed awkwardly.

"And what does he say about me?" Leeming inquired.

"It's not what he says—it's what he feels."

"What's that?"

"You frighten him."

Leeming was unsure of which way to deal with this. "Frighten?"

"He talks of an Army mission. He's a very brave boy but he's worried, which means the mission must be extremely dangerous. Yes?"

"I don't know anything about a mission." Leeming's mind was working fast on calculations about Caswell's indiscretion in discussing or even hinting at an Army mission. He decided Caswell was unlikely to have been dangerously indiscreet with details. He wondered too why she was questioning him almost as if Caswell wasn't present, like a mother discussing the welfare of her child with a schoolteacher in the child's presence. He felt there might lie a clue in that thought, or the beginnings of some clue as to why this attractive, sophisticated woman could have become involved with someone like Caswell. Leeming could now feel the fatigue of the Atlantic plane journey overtaking him. He should be in his hotel bed, but he was intrigued. He wanted a little more time to work out how she could have taken up with Caswell.

They stayed at the apartment for another twenty minutes and a second drink. The butler brought their coats and they headed out into the street. Caswell started darting in and out of the traffic from one side of the road to the other and finally collared a cab. The lieutenant gave the address of a club, and they all piled in.

It was eleven P.M. before a pattern emerged in their

meandering progress across Paris. Caswell was making all the decisions about where to go. He spent a lot of money on too much wine with an already expensive meal at Lasserre's. Then on to La Coupole for coffee. Then the Folies-Bergère for a show, then more clubs down Pigalle. The Paris that Caswell was showing them was the tourist Paris—beating the path unerringly to all the obvious places. Leeming wondered if at some point in the night they'd end up on the Tour Eiffel. They did.

Leeming and Lara were sitting at a table by a window overlooking the catwalk of the *deuxième étage*, and Caswell was at the bar organizing drinks, when Lara spoke quietly to Leeming. "He's a very fine boy."

"What's your definition?" Leeming asked.

She looked at him puzzled.

"I'm interested in why he attracts you?"

She had presumably worked it out for herself already, but she waited a moment before she spoke. "Stephen comes into my life and he threatens a terrible man in a wine and spirits store. And he takes me out to dinner and he talks twenty to the dozen and he tells me old corny jokes but he cheers me up. And we meet again the next day, and the next. And then the fourth night we both drink too much and he starts to talk, but really talk. He tells me something happened in the Army, in the Vietnamese civil war—he won't tell me what. But I've never seen anyone so vulnerable. And nothing is faked. This boy cries out in his sleep. Do you know what it was that happened to him in that war?"

Leeming shook his head. "No. I don't."

There was silence a moment while she tried to work out whether he was telling the truth or being discreet.

"What does he mean to you?" Leeming's words were softly probing.

"I have been living for seven years as a mistress of a man who gives me a lot of money so that once a week he can come to me and moan for an entire evening about how cruelly life has treated him—one of the most pampered men in France. I meet Stephen. Here is a boy who really lives in some private hell. I try to comfort him. Helping Stephen begins to justify my taking money from Franjou."

They went on from the Eiffel Tower to some night-clubs in Montmartre. It was working out to be a relaxing evening. For a period while Caswell drank himself into drunkenness he was the perfect unobtrusive host, leaving Leeming to the more or less undivided attention of Lara.

Leeming found it easy to talk to her. He thought back and realized it had been years since he'd met a woman whose company he could really relax in. There was an ordnance colonel's wife back at Fort Hood—a breezy little blonde with a gently amused nature. Lara of course was entirely different, obviously highly intelligent and aware. Intuitively he felt she had suffered a lot in her private life.

They ended up at a discotheque in Montparnasse. Lara saw some acquaintances at a corner table. She said they were too boring to be invited to join them, but she must go over and talk briefly with them. As soon as she left the table Leeming said, "You'll report at the Army and Navy gymnasium at eight A.M."

The alcohol was now beginning to get to Caswell—releasing the beginnings of aggression. "I don't know if you know it," he said acidly, looking at his watch, "that's in six hours from now."

"That's right."

Caswell snorted and left the table with a remark that he was going to request some proper music. He set off unsteadily toward a girl in a glass booth who was selecting the records.

Lara came back. She sat and said nothing for a moment and then she saw Caswell, having bribed some Country and Western music out of the girl in the booth, starting to head back unsteadily for their table. She suddenly leaned across and spoke softly and urgently to Leeming. "Please promise you will do something for me."

"Yes?"

"Take care of Stephen. Take care and protect him."

Leeming was a little surprised. "Sure. He'll be fine."

A few minutes later he got up to go. Caswell had insisted Lara stay on to hear out the jangling rhythms of the records he'd selected.

"I hope I meet you again," she said and leaned across the table and touched Leeming's hand.

"Yes," he said. "I hope we do."

"Why not one more goddam drink?" Caswell glowered at him.

"Listen to the music," Leeming ordered. "Then get to bed." He gave a last look to Lara and moved through the dancers and out into the night.

8

"THE PAPA-SAN CAME TO Paris from Saigon twenty years ago. The Mama-san came originally from Hue."

The fresh-faced Vietnamese man who made the introductions was in his forties. In the car going from the gymnasium to Odéon, he had told Leeming and Caswell that three years before he had been the principal special adviser to the French Consulate in Saigon. Leeming had met some consular special advisers in 'Nam. As a group they had always been particularly bright and usually treacherous. There had been a running scandal that many of the special advisers to foreign embassies supplemented their income by passing on all gathered intelligence to the CIA.

Caswell shook the old woman's hand. Leeming copied him. The Vietnamese started talking among themselves, not in Vietnamese but in French, so Leeming was able to follow some of it. The ex-special adviser was saying here was Lieutenant Caswell, the famous soldier who had killed communists at Da Loc and had been punished so unfairly by his own people.

The Papa-san and Mama-san were nodding. They remembered Da Loc and what had happened to the soldiers who had taken part. There was unmistakable sympathy for Caswell in their eyes.

They were in the rue Casimir Delavigne, a few hundred yards from the Ecole de Medicine, an area known locally and inaccurately as Chinatown. Vietnamese are not of Chinese stock and resent any suggestion that they are. The Vietnamese enclave in Paris in the Sixth Arrondissement is circumscribed by the half-dozen back streets off Odéon. Here live ten thousand or so procapitalist, pro-French, ex-Vietnamese nationals.

The ex-Saigon consulate adviser was named Trinh Giai. He had arrived at the gymnasium at eleven o'clock and had brought his own Renault. In the car, Caswell voiced some worries to Giai about his reception.

"No, mister, you understand my people spend their entire life fighting and killing communists. To them, you were in Da Loc where many communists were killed. You are a hero."

Caswell had looked dubiously at Leeming. Trinh Giai had intercepted the look. "I assure you," the young Vietnamese said, "these people are your friends."

It looked like it. Trinh Giai first took them to see a half-dozen of the best known older members of the community, and then the apartments of some of the younger exiles. The pattern of each meeting was identical. Caswell was introduced as one of the heroes of Da Loc. Then the Vietnamese adviser told the story about how Caswell's life was in danger. He was now living in Paris and had been threatened by some unidentified revenging force from the new communist homeland of Vietnam. All were asked to look out for any new Vietnamese faces within the Paris Indochinese community. Everyone they met responded in a positive manner.

It took three hours to tour the community, then they left Giai and headed for the American Embassy where they picked up Sergeant Simson. Mackerras had decided that Caswell needed a twenty-four-hour professional bodyguard. Leeming heard the news from Mackerras's secretary—he had not been consulted.

Simson was six-foot-three, and formidable. Everything about him was large including the bulge under his left arm where he kept his Magnum.

It had been a curious experience for Leeming to have met the Paris Vietnamese with Caswell in the role of hero. Or had everyone thought of him as such? It only needed one who shared the outrage of the rest of the world. Given ten thousand exiles, and even suppose that most of them had been in Paris for the last twenty years, still Leeming felt that there could be at least one among that number who might be a "sleeper," a spy who would this day be passing the word along that the American target was in Paris.

9

BUCKMAN SIPPED MORNING COFFEE and glanced impatiently once more at the clock in the all-white room in the Phillips' laboratories in West Berlin. It said ten-forty. The general was forty minutes late. He considered telling the white-coated technician standing in front of the video decks at the other end of the long room to go ahead, but decided it might be a complicated procedure to rewind the tapes to repeat the viewing. Then he thought he might phone Tempelhof. There was slight fog outside his hotel window on the Kaiserdam this morning. Maybe the airfield was fogged in.

Just as he was about to dial the general walked in the door, giving Buckman the barest nod, as if it were Buckman who had been late, Buckman for whom Mackerras and the technician had been waiting. The general took a seat facing the two large Tannoy speakers, with his back to his ADC.

They had both seen sections of the raw video recordings before the Phillips' technicians had gotten their hands on them. They had been more or less indecipherable, save for a few odd frames and none of those contained a picture of Van Dhoc. Now they were seeing the treated film, the ultraviolet light videotape recordings that had been taken with adapted Phillips two-inch orthicon TV cameras, nine weeks ago at the Gaber family residence near Montgomery, Alabama. The equipment had been developed toward the end of the war in Vietnam. It consisted of a series of linked video camera transmitters, each with a power source of ultraviolet light. In Vietnam they had been secretly placed at night on main routes, like Highway 19, transmitting to video recorders. One recorder and six cameras secreted away in trees or on rooftops were in many cases better than a half-dozen military patrols. After functioning through the night the tapes could be played back the following morning. Any movement on Highway 19 which had lasted longer than five minutes would be recorded. Army Intelligence had expected similar results at the Gaber house—hoping either to catch Van Dhoc on camera reconnoitering the house, or to tape some part of his actual murderous assault.

Each night at eleven P.M. when the household was settling down for sleep, the two master sergeants who were to die with the Gabers switched on the video equipment which was secreted in a tool cupboard in a garage. The garage was chosen because it was separate from the house—a necessary precaution because in all the other murders the house had been burned down.

The killings of the Gaber family and the two master sergeants took place, the house was incendiarized, and the garage was untouched. Experts from Army Intelligence arrived at the still-smoking ruins in Montgomery and took the video equipment off to Fort Holabird. At Holabird the six videotapes covering the six hours of recording that night were played back. The tapes added up to one gray-black continuous snowstorm. The video equipment had obviously broken down. Routinely the tapes were sent to Holland for examination by Phillips, Eindhoven, the manufacturers. Phillips' initial reaction was that, contrary to the instructions supplied, the VCR in the garage had been set up next to some equipment emitting a strong magnetic field. Army Intelligence technicians returned to the Gaber garage. There was nothing in the building that could have provided such a field. Fort Holabird concluded that some unfathomable accident had happened, and that was the end of the story. Much to their surprise, two weeks later Phillips had come back to them with the information that as the waveband interference had been consistent, there was a chance of reprocessing the videotapes to try to bring out some pictures. Two weeks after that, Phillips announced they had found some faint pictures and, unbelievably, some recognizable shots of a man. Mackerras in Paris was put in touch with Phillips in Eindhoven and received black-and-white photos of the footage. He then requested to view all the reconstituted tape in Holland. Phillips suggested he might care to look at it in Berlin.

The technician turned to General Mackerras. *"Sind sie fertig?"*

"Ja."

The man hovered over the decks and pressed the "replay" on four tape decks. With a number of scratches and static sound a picture came up on a monitor in the middle of the long console. The technician had already been through the tapes. There were only three minutes on one and thirty-four seconds on the other showing Van Dhoc.

Buckman and Mackerras's eyes were frozen on the monitor. The picture displayed was pale gray. It showed the man, then, clearly, his face, as he came stealthily through the trees approaching the Gaber house. He walked carefully, almost as if he knew unseen lumens of ultraviolet light were placing his murderer's image for perpetuity on a piece of tape.

Buckman and Mackerras studied Dhoc's movements past the two cameras and around the house. Buckman wondered what his general was thinking. Was the Berlin trip to see this footage a waste of time? No, Mackerras was a perfectionist. He was on a mission to hunt this man down—if there was some video of the quarry, he'd want to see it. And apparently see it over again. The technician had turned to the general. *"Noch einmal?"* he asked.

Mackerras nodded, and settled back in his seat.

Buckman concentrated on the monitor, not just to view the pictures again, but to use them as a focus for his thoughts. He wasn't too interested in shots of Van Dhoc. What interested him was the problem that had now been passed over. How had the tapes been ruined? How had a strong magnetic field appeared where there was no such field? Buckman's mind concentrated as the gray-mist pictures of Van Dhoc came back on the monitor. His mind could not gloss over an interrogative as large as the one posed by the ruined tapes. He had always found in life there was an explanation for everything—it was simply a question of where and how intently you looked for it.

10

BUCKMAN ARRIVED BACK IN Paris at eight P.M. Mackerras had caught a USAF mail plane four hours earlier.
Buckman picked up his boyfriend at the university and
took him for a meal at Laperouse. They went straight
from the restaurant home to a shower and bed. But he
did not sleep.

The boyfriend, called Tod, was twenty-six and
snored. The colonel had met him first in the coffee shop
at the Sorbonne, where Tod was studying modern lan-
guages. A good-looking boy, and bright. Buckman did
not believe he was a practicing homosexual, just a
young person a little confused about his sexual identity
and needing a roof over his head. For the past two
months he'd provided the boy with that.

The bedroom of the apartment in rue Faubourg St.
Honoré was small, the bed pushed against the wall. He
had a problem getting out of it without waking the boy.
Then he thought maybe he would wake Tod. He needed
to talk it out with someone, verbalize unformed ideas,
and get another view on the videotapes he'd seen in
Berlin. Of course he would express the problem in such
a way that there would be no breech of security—and
maybe the boy knew something about electronics. He
debated, then decided against waking Tod. He succeeded in getting out of bed without doing so.

He was naked and the apartment cold. He shivered
himself into underpants and vest, put on a robe and
slippers and shuffled out of the bedroom, across the lit-

tle baroque and brocade living room filled with bad antiques, and into the tiny kitchen. He ran the tap into the
percolator, lit the gas with a match, and came back into
the living room and pulled the curtains.

The wet roofs of the gray day greeted him. A garbage
truck made its way along the empty streets below, two
figures shrouded in its cab. And a taxi, maybe carrying
a lover back to the solace of a bed in which to sleep. He
himself felt tired. After Laperouse there'd been a couple
of athletic and exhausting sex bouts but even while
these were going on he had been thinking about the
videotapes.

He knew one of the master sergeants from Fort Holabird who had died with the Gabers. A big, intelligent
guy called Perrin. The Phillips technician had said that
the interference that had nearly obliterated the tape
could have been caused for example by the close proximity of an arcing electric light bulb—but he doubted
that an arcing electric light bulb would last as
long as the six hours' duration of the tapes. What else
could have caused the interference? Buckman had
asked the technician, and got the answer—an electric
motor or motors, relays, or solenoids in very close proximity to the video recorder. But Perrin and his col-
league, who started the video machines every night, had
been supplied with precise instructions about sensitivity
problems. The question was, would someone like Sergeant Perrin carry out to the letter his instructions?
Buckman knew the answer was yes.

Pursuing that line there must have been something in
that garage that Perrin and his partner never saw.
Something subsequently neutralized before the electronic
experts from Fort Holabird arrived on the scene. Some
other motors, solenoids, servos. Now what kind of removable box of tricks would contain any or all of those
items, Buckman wondered . . . apart from say another VCR receiver. He'd seen the inside of a Phillips
VCR—it was full of motors and servos. . . .

Buckman never drank the coffee that was percolating
in his kitchen. He picked up the phone and dialed the

number of General Mackerras' private apartment in rue
Gautier.

The general's voice came on the line, snappy with
sleep. "Yes?"

"Buckman. I've been working with the problem of
the interference on those videotapes, sir. I think I've got
the answer. I'd like us to meet urgently."

"I don't know if you know it, son," the general
growled, "but it's twenty after five."

"General, I wouldn't wake you unless I had important
news. And I'm afraid it's bad. I believe the interference
on those tapes was caused by the fact that there were
two video machines in that garage. One was ours. My
belief is that the other was secretly placed there by another Intelligence agency. And that being the case, I
suspect our whole fucking project is about to go down
the toilet, sir. . . ."

11

Six days passed, Sunday through Saturday, as Leeming continued Caswell's training. Days when he felt a sense of alienation—maybe because it was a passage of time spent solely on physical things. But there were other reasons for his feeling of detachment. A foreign city in the no-man's-land of a suite in the George V. Nothing in that expensive suite to identify his recent life with. And now he was back in his former life—in the Army again— up at five A.M., dressed quickly, and straight into a cab for Avenue Wagram to pick up Caswell for a two-hour workout at the gymnasium. Then breakfast. This was Marine style, workout first, breakfast after. A shock to the system after two years of the gentle coma of day-to-day existence on the farm. There was a final element in his feeling of separateness from events, the continuing growing presentiment that Caswell would not make the grade. If he was now asked his opinion he would say no, Caswell was not capable of a successful initiative in Albania. But he had not been asked for his opinion. He had begun to wonder if he ever would be.

He had a nose for the interior person—feelings necessarily hard to define although he wrestled with himself for definitions. It had nothing to do with his experience, instant value judgments frequently shown to be right. Not that, but the experience of battle, of running that Special Forces Camp in 'Nam, of looking at soldiers and knowing which of the bright-faced ones had the smell of death about them, and which were the ones you could count on to survive. He'd had certain feelings about Caswell the moment he'd set eyes on him. By Friday the host of intuitions were beginning to cement into a decision he might have to make, to face the general and tell him to find another recruit. Then suddenly on Friday Caswell told him why he wanted the mission.

They'd reached the six-mile point when Caswell unexpectedly slowed up, shook his head and sat down heavily on a park bench.

"On your feet," Leeming commanded sharply, marking time on the spot.

"Too much. Rest."

"Get up."

"I have to rest." Caswell said it loudly.

Leeming didn't have the breath to argue. He sat down beside Caswell.

Across the park on a path beneath some elm trees, two old men, looking like clochards, swept leaves into piles in a semicircle around a wire basket smoldering with the dead harvest of last autumn. Their movements slow motion, like zombies, as if their orders were not to finish the task until next autumn's fallout reinstated their employment. Caswell was studying the old men. He was silent for a moment, forming his thoughts. Then he spoke.

"Colonel, I'm worried. I know unless I get your approval, I don't get this mission."

"Why d'you say that?"

"I've known right from the start General Mackerras has other guys up his sleeve."

Leeming didn't know that.

"I have to kill this Van Dhoc. Give me the chance."

"It's not up to me."

"Don't bullshit me. I know your brief. For Jimmy Holby, David Krantz, Captain Gaber, I have to carry out this mission."

Leeming said nothing, knew that Caswell had arrived at a point where he had to verbalize his feelings. So far he'd made no mention of the murders of his friends.

"It wasn't said at the court-martial. These things aren't

said. Holby and Krantz were closer to me than anyone in my life. You should understand. You were there. You know what it's like. You must have experienced it yourself, dozens of S and D patrols, sitting up there in a Chinook with all the hardware in the world, M60's, M79's, but you're as easy to hit as a cloud. I remember every one of those two-hour rides. Every second day the same mission. And you are dying along with guys who are breathing this second but in eternity the next. We lived in each other's pockets, Beta Company, 2nd Battalion. We loved each other more than brothers. And some of us returned from our hundred and fifty Search-and-Destroy actions. Holby, Krantz and me always returned. We were indestructible. Our method was simple—kill so fucking hard and fast there's no VC ever gets the chance to get a bead on. That was why we survived. Then one day, one out of a hundred and fifty missions, there were twenty whole minutes of fucking madness, and okay, the innocent died. So they say."

Leeming was looking away from him across the grass to the old men on their snail-slow sweep.

"You listening, Colonel?" Caswell's tone was sharp. Leeming nodded. "Fuck it, we know what we did. But let me tell you, everyone who died in 'Nam, the peasants or our boys, died in the overall massacre, no better or worse than Da Loc. And as pointless." Caswell's voice was low and hard. "I'll tell you something else, Colonel—something I've never told anyone before. When I was standing in the center of Da Loc, with Krantz and Holby, and we were mowing them down as they ran off through the goddam compounds, you know what I was thinking? I was thinking we're not killing enough! We're not getting them all! We'll have to do an RK on this village! I'll have to make out a report recommending an RK on this place. You know what 'RK' meant?"

"ReKill," Leeming said softly.

"Right. I was thinking I'll recommend an RK on Da Loc. We'll come back unexpectedly in two or three days and shoot the rest. Too many have got away. And I should have done that. Because you know who's handling the RK now on Da Loc? Yeah, there's a man out there doing the ReKill and his name is Van Dhoc. And for the sake of my murdered buddies I'm telling you that you have to recommend me because I have to get him if it's the last fucking thing I do on this earth."

12

MACKERRAS' OFFICE LAID ON two more visits to the Vietnamese community with the same chaperon, Trinh Giai. Caswell, Leeming and the Marine bodyguard Simson trooped along on the tour of introductions, nodding into smiling faces, accepting tea and the gentle questionings of the elders. By the second trip Caswell was finding it difficult to keep up a front, and Leeming realized that Caswell probably didn't like Vietnamese people. In view of his history Leeming decided that conclusion might seem a little overly obvious.

Leeming had always liked the Vietnamese and he liked these exiles in particular. With their average two decades in France, they were greatly different from the culturally Americanized Vietnamese he'd met during the war. They also appeared to fit easily into Paris. The Parisians, ever fast to devalue other races like Algerians and East Africans, evidently had a lot of time for the citizens of a country whose war had claimed many among two generations of its St. Cyr officers and men. The Paris Vietnamese lived their private lives apart, kept their culture, but at the same time were now an integral part of the hard-nosed world of Paris business.

On Thursday, Caswell was obviously tired from his workout at the gymnasium. He eyed Leeming circumspectly all morning and then, either out of guilt or mischief, told him that the previous night, against orders, he'd seen Lara, and spent the night with her.

Leeming had been anticipating challenges to his authority, and was not concerned with this one, but registered an official protest. Caswell shrugged off his own omissions, then added, "She particularly asked me to pass on regards and things. You could do okay there."

"What do you mean by that?" Leeming asked coolly.

"I don't claim exclusive rights. How can I? I'm poaching from the little guy—Franjou. So call her."

"I'm in Paris to plan an important mission. I've no time for anything but the mission. That should be your conclusion too."

"Sometimes I wonder if you're human, Colonel, sir."

Leeming let that go. He didn't want to start any row which just might escalate into his revealing to the lieutenant that he was becoming more and more certain that Caswell was the wrong man for the mission. It was difficult to put his finger on specific reasons for this. One worry was that all of Caswell's responses were emotional—that the reason he wanted to go after Van Dhoc was "for the sake of my murdered buddies"—and not for the practical reason that he happened to be on Van Dhoc's death list. This removed him one step from reality, and that condition would not be affordable once he got to Albania. Finally it must be apparent that in the years since Da Loc, Caswell had not grown in wisdom or maturity. The problem with Caswell was still the original unresolved position that the lieutenant would never have become involved in this mission if his actions and reactions in the village of Da Loc had been sensible. Leeming decided he must organize a more searching investigation into critical flaws in Caswell's personality. He phoned Mackerras' office and told him he was running a final test on Caswell. The general listened in silence and made only one comment to the effect that couldn't these kinds of games go wrong? Leeming gave his opinion that it was possible, but he felt justified in the circumstances. The general thought about it for a moment and agreed to lay on a para-drop.

13

THEY WERE ABOUT THIRTY miles south of Paris. The plane climbed through a layer of cumulus to about ten thousand feet and found clean air. Leeming looked out of the navigator's window. Visibility looked good for the jump.

They were in a small twin-engined AFF Breguet 401. There were four of them—pilot, navigator, Caswell and himself. They were sitting on thinly padded seats in the front of the bulbous pod of fuselage. Behind them was a clearway to the rear-opening jump doors. Leeming leaned forward and asked the pilot to take the craft on another ten miles and pointed southwest, where he'd spotted a cloudless horizon.

The pilot wheeled the plane round to its new course, opened the throttle and pulled it up at the same time. They started the last climb. Leeming had requested a ceiling of fifteen thousand feet. The parachute jump he'd planned would have ten thousand feet of free fall. He tapped Caswell on the shoulder and indicated he should leave his seat and move to the rear compartment. Caswell nodded. He seemed calm and collected enough. He slipped out of his safety belt and squeezed down the tight passageway between the seats, into the kitting and jump area.

The compartment could hold six outfitted men and instructor. Caswell, as soon as he'd gotten into the compartment, had gone straight to his parachute and started to pile it on his back. Leeming stopped him, indicating for him to put the chute down, and then to sit. There were two three-seater benches on each side of the aft cockpit.

"I want you to listen to me for a minute, and no comments. Clear?" Leeming said, his voice loud to compensate for the aircraft noise.

Caswell nodded. He had made para-drops before. He looked confident.

"The general gave me two weeks with you. I think physically you're okay. There's one thing you have to have enough of on this mission—guts. There's a test which has been used unofficially in Marine training."

Caswell looked as if he couldn't connect Leeming's words with the business at hand. He was sitting forward on the bench, fairly close to Leeming. The motion of the plane moved the two men together.

"You querying my courage, Colonel?"

"Not querying, testing. I want to find its breaking point. The general agrees to this test."

Caswell said nothing.

"A minute and this plane will be at fifteen thousand. You and I are going to jump. We're going to free fall ten thousand. I'm going to have two parachutes on. You're going to have no parachute. At five thousand feet I'll grab you and open both chutes—you hold on to me tight."

Sudden suspicion on Caswell's face turned quickly to incomprehension and anger. "Walk out with no chute?"

Leeming nodded slowly.

"No." Caswell said it softly. "To jump without a chute, no way."

"Have one of those lousy French cigarettes of yours. I'll go forward. I'll be back in two minutes."

Leeming moved back to the cockpit, squeezed himself past some radio equipment and into his seat. The plane was leveling now. He put his head close to the window. A half-dozen miles in front of him the clouds started to break up and he could see the patchwork of the winter-brown French fields spread to the horizon. The navigator turned with a query in his look. When

Leeming nodded, he went back to his map for a fix on the nearest airfield over which Leeming and the lieutenant could drop, and where the Breguet could land to pick them up. He found a reference and exchanged words with the pilot.

Leeming felt a tap on his shoulder. He turned. Caswell stood there. The color had drained from his face. "Okay."

Leeming moved quickly past Caswell to the back of the plane. He started to strap on the two parachutes, one front and one on his back. It took him a minute. He didn't look at Caswell while he checked and adjusted the straps and his reach to the rip cords. He realized that Caswell too would be checking that he was making the right moves. Then he finished and looked up.

He could see that Caswell was almost on the point of hesitation, but then gave a short nod. Leeming turned and shouted to the pilot indicating the doors. The pilot sat forward and pressed the servos. The little Breguet decompressed quickly and unfussily. Leeming felt his ears go, but no other discomfort. The pilot released the rear doors, and slowly they began to swing open to reveal the emptiness of sky and the last of the cumulus clouds turning from cotton sheet into strips and wisps below. And below that, the fields, fifteen thousand feet down.

There was no chance now for further words. Wind roar as the doors opened pitched to a high and violent whistling accompanied by a buffeting that was making the Breguet pendulum slowly from side to side as it wallowed down the sky. Its speed eased from a cruising two hundred to a drop speed of a little over a hundred.

Leeming did it by signals. The white-faced Caswell was nodding sharply as if anxious, now his mind was made up, to show his willingness, as if guilty that he had first refused. Leeming clipped his chute guide to the overhead rail, took Caswell's hand and slowly the two men inched toward the door, Leeming's left hand gripping the lieutenant's right and Leeming's right hand gripping the side handrails. They approached the jump gate.

Leeming turned and waited. The navigator signaled with a wave. Leeming said it, shouted it, "Once out, spread arms . . ." He demonstrated, opening his arms wide. "On the three count. . . . One . . ." He turned and looked at Caswell, testing the final hesitation on the lieutenant's face. "Two . . ." It was critical that they both jumped within a second of each other. "Three!" For a split second Caswell hesitated, Leeming gave him a pull, and they were out, and slicing wind down the iced and empty sky, the plane suddenly fast and far from them, like they had never been on it, like it had never held them to that secure distance between heaven and earth.

Leeming's arms crucified out, trying, as he fell, to adjust his body altitude in the frozen air, the second-by-second change of altitude crackling his ears and pounding the blood to his brain, aware that he must use arms and legs to bring about more deceleration. He was more heavily built and weighted with twin parachutes. Caswell above him, maybe twenty feet above him, with his back to him, his hands flapping ineffectively, having forgotten that he could use the direction of the flat of his palm to rotate his body, but nonetheless succeeding in presenting enough down windage that there could be a problem in Leeming leveling with the man in time, that is before five thousand feet.

Leeming looked down. The French countryside sprawled out below them, a model in miniature built for a rich child's toy. Dark brown and black fields, and some level stubble—it all looked suitable as a landing site. Leeming looked up. Caswell, by instinct or otherwise, had remembered, or gotten the hang of it, and had turned his body, stabilized the spin with his outstretched palms, and was now six feet above Leeming and looking down. "This is where it happens," Leeming thought to himself. "Past the shock of cold air. Now fear, vertigo. Then panic . . ." Leeming paddled arms and legs out and, using hands as ailerons to move himself closer to the lieutenant, looked up the six feet that separated them.

He was crying, but unseen tears that were torn away from red eyes by the hurl of the slipstream. That was for ten seconds. Then he started to scream, scream so loud that the noise could penetrate the shriek of air over Leeming's ears, and be registered on popping eardrums.

He tried to clutch down at Leeming, but Leeming used his hands to glide his motionless body a few feet farther away from the plummeting man. Caswell was in full panic and thrashing about like a lunatic, making desperate lunges to grab Leeming and missing, and spiraling with his body across Leeming's glide path but never near enough to catch him.

Then Caswell's face was contorted into one long rending howl as he saw death as an inevitable fact, saw that Leeming for some reason was killing him, had confidence-tricked him into this violent suicide trip through the sky.

And Leeming, suspended in space, looked into the lieutenant's screaming face floating toward him, then away, and he wondered if in some way it would be kinder to let Caswell fall unchecked and die. Because the lieutenant might find it hard to live with the real knowledge of himself, that he had made that fatal mistake of pitching his bravura so loud it had, up to this moment, drowned out the doubts he must have had about himself.

It had taken thirty-five seconds. They were down to three thousand feet. Leeming could see the little airport of Bretagny, three miles from the nearest main town of Clairefontaine. There was a large farmhouse about a half a mile north of their falling bodies. He would aim for the farmhouse and hope it had a phone to call the airport. Caswell was in level fall with him, now screaming soundlessly, just the face torn in the contortion of his nightmare. No attempt at control at all—he would be hysterical now until his feet actually touched ground.

Leeming felt a last stab of guilt about the finality of the experiment. But it had made the point. As far as he was concerned, Caswell was unsuitable for a complex, important and dangerous mission.

14

HE'D LEFT CASWELL AT the airport. From the moment he'd grabbed him at three thousand feet, pulled rip cords, released the two parachutes and fallen to a gentle landing, and throughout the long wait in the farmhouse for transport, and through the short hop in the Breguet back to Orly, Caswell had said little more than a few monosyllables. But he had cried silently on the plane from Bretagny to Orly. At Orly he'd walked ahead of Leeming to the Aeroclub's exit, waved down a cab, and gone off without a backward glance.

Leeming found a phone at the Aeroclub and called SHAPE Headquarters. General Mackerras, he was told, was at a meeting, but the secretary had a word with him and returned to the phone with the message that the general would see him at the George V at eight o'clock. Leeming took a cab from Orly back to the hotel, showered, dressed, and had one Scotch sent to his room. It was seven-thirty.

The general arrived promptly at eight. It took Leeming five minutes to describe the para-drop, giving his conclusion that Caswell was the wrong man for a high-risk mission. The general nodded a few times, made some noncommittal statements, mentioned he had a date with the American ambassador, and said there would be further discussions about it tomorrow.

"Did the mission hang on Caswell, sir?" Leeming asked.

"No, no," the general said offhandedly. "He was one possible. There are others. That is not to say I've agreed to junk him."

Leeming had dinner sent up to his suite, read a copy of *Newsweek* from cover to cover, and decided to go to bed early. He was asleep by nine-thirty. The phone rang at seven minutes past five. He opened his eyes and studied the dismal Paris morning outside the windows of his cold suite. He gave himself five seconds to clear his head, then picked it up.

"Leeming, it's Buckman. I'll have a car to you in ten minutes. Go to the general's office, SHAPE, and wait there."

"What's happening?"

"You'll find out."

"Tell me what's happening," Leeming said firmly, a reasonable question from one ordered out of bed at five A.M. Anyhow he could detect something wrong in Buckman's voice.

"Caswell . . ." Buckman seemed to hesitate to add more, "he's dead."

"What d'you mean dead?"

"Van Dhoc. Murdered."

"What?"

"Murdered."

"For God's sake, when? How? Wasn't Simson with him all night?"

Buckman either didn't think there was any relevance in a post-mortem, or maybe he had others to phone. The phone went down on Leeming's questions.

Leeming got out of bed and dressed quickly. The Army chauffeur was already in the lobby when he stepped out of the elevator minutes later and identified himself. The soldier gave a smart salute. They walked through the foyer and passages and left the hotel by the west entrance. He got into the car. The chauffeur went around and climbed into the front.

"Take me to fourteen Avenue Wagram."

The sergeant driver turned and looked at him. "I

got orders to take you to General Mackerras' office."

"After Wagram, fourteen Avenue Wagram."

The driver shrugged and started the car. "If I get problems, I quote you, sir."

"Yes, I'm giving you an order."

There were two U.S. Military Chevrolets pulled into the curb outside the high building on Avenue Wagram when Leeming's car arrived. He had only been to Caswell's apartment twice before. There was a gendarme in the hall where the concierge normally loitered. The policeman stopped him as he crossed from the car and was heading into the building.

"Où allez-vous?"

"Colonel Leeming, U.S. Army. I understand there's been an accident."

"Attendez." The gendarme took his hand from the butt of his revolver where it was resting, and an index finger stroked up the score of entry phone buttons. He selected a button near the top and pressed it. A moment later there was a click, and the metallic voice of Buckman out of the entry phone speaker.

"Oui?"

"It's me, Leeming."

There was a silence of some seconds while Buckman worked out whether he should conduct an inquiry over the door phone into why Leeming had not gone to the general's office. He decided against it.

"Sixième étage."

Leeming nodded to the gendarme and stepped past him and across the uneven terrazzo floor to the open door of the old wire-cage elevator. On the sixth floor there was another gendarme. The man didn't challenge him. Leeming walked past him, through the open door into the apartment. Buckman was standing in the hall. Also in the hall was Simson's body. The sergeant was lying, head close to the wall, and on his back. Leeming could see the entry hole of a large-caliber bullet on the left side of his neck. The bullet had been angled down into the chest and toward the heart. No exit point visible. A straightforward professional execution.

Leeming stood up and took one step toward the living room. Buckman intercepted him.

"What d'you want?"

"To see Caswell."

"Take my advice," Buckman's voice was low and sure. "Change your mind."

"I've had as much active service as you, Colonel."

Buckman snapped back, "God help you if you've ever seen anything like this."

Leeming's view through the door was of roughly half the area of the room beyond. Four French police were in the room, trench coats still on, their faces pale and unshaven. A photographer with an expensive Hasselblad was taking pictures. The other men were lounging around as if they already knew that in an hour from now phone calls from the State Department, Washington, would kill this investigation and any publicity about it as stone dead as the victims themselves. It would be listed as suicide, a difficult proposition to sell since the second victim would never have been able to perform the mutilations suffered. Nonetheless suicide it would be. There were no journalists from the murder-hungry Paris newspapers in the damp street below. Leeming walked into the room, and saw the reason for the white faces, the desultory talk.

Caswell was stripped to the waist, naked except for pajama trousers, sitting upright at a desk. The knife wound that had killed him was a suture about two inches across, midway down his back. The blood from the wound had poured down to soak most of his pants and trickle onto the carpet.

Around the head was a huge towel, also soaked in blood. Leeming slipped past the uninquiring eyes of the French cops. His stomach turned over. It was not as he had at first thought. The terrycloth on the neck was just a bunched-up towel. The lieutenant's head had been completely severed from the body and thrown into a wastepaper basket next to the desk. Caswell's eyes were still open and angled up looking almost directly at Leeming.

Leeming felt vomit rise in his throat. He rallied his will, and he was over it, although there was cold sweat suddenly in every pore of his body. He looked from the head in the wastepaper basket to the bunched-up blood-heavy towel balanced precariously on the stub of the neck.

He turned. Buckman was standing just behind him. He saw Leeming's look, knew he was demanding an explanation. For a moment the other man said nothing. Everyone had made a series of calculations with no room for error, and there had been a terrible error.

"What does the towel mean?" Leeming's voice was hard.

"Did you ever read the full transcript, the Da Loc court-martial?"

"Not a full transcript," Leeming answered.

"I think the explanation of the towel comes from something said at the Court."

"What?"

"During the trial one of the officers, I don't remember which one—it wasn't Caswell, anyhow he was asked how he knew he'd only killed half a dozen gooks at Loc. He said because he'd only had a dozen clips for his M16. It was suggested that was enough ammo to kill a hundred. He said no—in one case he'd fired a whole clip into one guy. He was asked to describe this. He said the guy was a typical VC who came to the village for recuperation. He described how the man had a cast around his head—the VC would take a regular towel, soak it in plaster of paris, wrap it and let it set around a broken arm, or a sprained shoulder. This guy may have had a dislocated neck. He was asked what was the effect of firing a full clip into the man. He said, 'It cut his head off at the neck. The head fell off his body, leaving the plaster towel still in position—a tent over the head, but no head.' "

Leeming took one last look at the bloodied head and the eyes still staring from the wastepaper basket and walked from the room. For the first time he realized that Van Dhoc was not a man simply bent on retribution, but on a psychopath's revenge. It also occurred to him forcefully that it was now his destiny to find this man and either destroy or be destroyed by him.

15

THE SUN CAME OUT for four days and Paris was gently embalmed in unseasonable warmth. Leeming took walks. He discovered the Jardin du Luxembourg, there and back, a useful exercise from the George V by way of Ile de la Cité. Buckman phoned him once, two days after the murder. The man had one question—had Leeming done any mountain climbing recently? He'd been fairly noncommittal, wondering if Buckman's question was just an opener for something else. It wasn't. Buckman had rung off with the answer that rock climbing had been part of Leeming's training curriculum in his Special Forces Camp. There was also a call from the general's office, but only to do with the mechanics of how to sign the bill at the hotel, and rent a car if he wanted. His wife used to play a trick—pretend every year that he'd forgotten their wedding anniversary. He'd arrive back at officers' quarters at Fort Hood to find his house stuffed with his brother officers and various relatives. He was supposed to show surprise and guilt. But of course he'd realized the preparations for days in advance. He felt this was happening now. And all he could do was wander the parks, sit on benches, and witness the visible thrusts of crocuses emerging from bare winter soil. He knew he had to accept—at least for a few days—a passive role.

On the fourth day, Friday, at eleven-thirty, he got a phone call from the general's secretary—would he go to le Louis XIV for lunch? The call sounded like an afterthought, the girl couched the question like he had the option to say no, he was too busy. But he knew this was the culmination. It had taken the four days since the murder for the general to reorchestrate the score, rewrite the memos, rework the policies and the politics to form new plans and get new assents. And he, Leeming, was obviously still included in those plans. He thought about that in the cab to Boulevard St. Denis—that Caswell's death had thrown open the options again. He could get out, he had every right to. But he knew that the answer was to carry on. Caswell had died but nothing had changed—except the reinforced resolution to find the man who'd executed the lieutenant.

The general wasn't at the restaurant. Buckman stood under the huge oak beams, in front of the fire grate, one log burning tamely. A man stood next to him talking quietly. He was around five-foot-seven, with a thin face, broad muscular shoulders, and slim hipped. He had thick eyebrows over darting blue eyes and was wearing an expensive gray suit. His age, Leeming calculated, as he moved in on the two, was around thirty-eight. He looked a hundred-percent fit. The contrast between the man and Buckman was particularly marked. Buckman looked positively pale. Whatever the general's new plan was, it had apparently involved the colonel in some exhausting days and sleepless nights.

Buckman introduced the man. "Spiro Jakova."

Leeming shook the hand. He felt the power of hard muscle there.

"John Leeming." Buckman completed the introduction as the maitre d' advanced with menus. He stopped the man as he started to hand the menus around. "We'll go straight to the table, Albert. Make it a quiet one."

"*Certainement,* Monsieur Buckman." The maitre d' led them out of the main room into an empty anteroom of half a dozen tables.

"No cocktails, some wine," Buckman suggested, and looked to the others for disagreement. They said nothing.

"I send the sommelier, sir."

They sat down at a table and for a moment there was silence. Then Buckman addressed Leeming. "Apologies from the general and myself that we weren't in touch. We've had plenty to do these last few days. We also had to locate Spiro here. And rethink the whole operation again. But we're back on the rails."

Leeming said nothing.

"Let me talk about Spiro." Buckman lit a cigarette, taking his time as if he was about to deliver an extensive lecture. "Born Tiranha, Albania, lives two or three months of the year in Albania, the rest in Greece or here in Paris. He's got two jobs. The first is a full-time occupation—he hates the Hoxha regime. The second is that he's a dealer in antiques or, as he puts it, a stealer of antiquities." He looked over to Jakova for agreement, but the man was studying the menu. "You may or may not know—I didn't—Albania is a treasure trove of Roman, Byzantine, Venetian and Turkish antiquities. Since the communists have gotten around to closing the churches, millions of dollars of religious art and objets have disappeared into the homes of the peasantry. Spiro ferrets the stuff out, smuggles it out of the country, sells it. It's big business."

Jakova was still studying the menu.

"It's a dangerous occupation. Spiro, tell Leeming here how many gun battles you had last year with the border police."

Jakova shrugged, looked around as if he was appealing to some other witnesses to say there was nothing very spectacular in shooting border police. "We shoot quite a few *policiza* last year."

Leeming was still weighing up appearances, the tall finely built body, its handsomeness somehow spoiled by the overgrowth of eyebrows, the expensive suit, large gold watch and silk shirt, but again the appearance faulted by the man's rough hands which had the broken fingernails of a professional rock climber.

Buckman went on. "Hoxha's political police have assassinated three members of his family, put six others in jail, including a half-brother. Spiro has every reason to want to support any attack against the regime. He's also a well-known figure among resistance fighters in Albania. He's prepared to accompany our appointed assassin into Albania, and also to form a group of people who will aid us in the goal to find Van Dhoc and kill him."

"Who's appointed to go into Albania to kill Dhoc?"

Buckman smiled thinly. "I thought you'd guessed. We're sending the man best qualified. That happens to be you."

He had guessed, and yet somehow the confirmation came as a surprise. "No comment about that yet. You go on. When did you say Mr. Jakova here was last back in Albania?"

"Spiro," the man corrected Leeming.

"Spiro." Leeming acknowledged the name.

The man looked up from his menu. "I was there three months ago."

"He had a close call," Buckman added. "Lost his transport. Had to walk the hundred miles up over the mountains into Greece."

Leeming pondered that. Perhaps Buckman was describing a remarkable achievement—that this man had walked through the mountains out of Albania. He'd been into the library at the George V and looked up Albania in the *Encyclopaedia Britannica,* and also studied closely a Rand McNally map. Leeming, well used to reading maps, had looked at the physical map of Albania and realized the reason why this communist country could laugh at Russia and go to bed with the Chinese—it had an unbroken wall of immense mountains all around its borders. The borders were the precipitous mountains—hundreds of miles of precipitous mountains. Yes, Buckman was describing an achievement when he said the man had walked and climbed a hundred miles through these mountains to escape.

"I always recommend one thing in this place, the *gigue de chevreuil,*" Buckman announced. Leeming felt that the other man changing the subject to food was an oblique way of telling him to hold back, the Albania discussion would be highly complex. It was going to take a long meal just to hammer out the initial pros and cons of any plan. But Leeming was also thinking about how this man, four days after the brutal murder and mutilation of Caswell, could be casually recommending specialities in an expensive restaurant.

Jakova had now picked up the wine list. Leeming's eyes were still on him. An antiques thief and part-time freedom fighter as the lynch-pin to the Mackerras plan somehow didn't have the right feel about it. He decided there must be other facets to Jakova that recommended him. Or perhaps there weren't and this was a hastily botched-up plan. He must remember the choice was still open, and his. And he should make it as simple as choosing one dish or rejecting another.

The maitre d' and the wine waiter arrived. Leeming wanted one course only, the other two a complex lunch and a fuss over the wine. The maitre d' and the sommelier departed. Leeming decided he'd ask some questions immediately. "You've run a security clear on Spiro?"

"He's clear," Buckman said.

"By inference you're saying it's 'Go' on the initiative?"

Buckman nodded.

"What reason have you to believe Dhoc returned to Albania after the Caswell execution?"

"We have a 'Van Dyke' A.M. on the morning of Caswell's killing, Alitalia, Paris to Venice. I'm sorry to say we had two G2 personnel at the airport but they were looking for Paris through to Trieste. Of course too late we realized Venice is as good or better a small-craft embarkation point for Albania."

Leeming held back a comment on the incompetence. "Any indication where Dhoc is in Albania?"

"The key question. No, we don't know where he is. But we do have the name of one man in Tiranha, the capital, who'll know exactly where he's located."

"What man?"

"Let's not rush. That's the meat of it. The query about the art of the possible."

Leeming let it go for the moment. "The outing. Myself, Spiro. Who else?"

"The Feiseler flyer, Meyer . . ."

"You?"

Buckman shook his head. "I don't think I'll be going. That could change."

"At the other end?"

"When the time comes, Spiro goes two days in front of you. He'll go to the capital and collect a dozen friends."

"Why?"

"You're going to need some help."

"Why?"

"Mackerras will tell you why."

Leeming turned to Jakova. "Who are these friends?"

"Freedom fighters. People whose families have suffered Hoxha too long."

"Reasons why these Albanians will want to help us find our man?" Leeming addressed the question to Jakova.

Buckman replied. "We're paying over some gold— thirty thousand dollars' worth—to help them finance the resistance fight inside their country. We're also sending arms and ammunition for a group of a dozen. They'll keep the arms to fight on after the job's over."

"Mercenaries." Leeming chewed on the word.

"No," Buckman said.

Leeming corrected. "Yes."

"The Mois warriors made the best fighting men in 'Nam. They hated us, they hated the VC. We paid cash."

Leeming said it gently. "We lost that war."

The conversation was interrupted by the arrival of the sommelier carrying a dust-gray bottle of claret. Buckman nodded at the label, tried a sample, then gave instructions to decant. The sommelier retreated.

Leeming meanwhile was still trying to come to some conclusion about the new man. Jakova didn't seem to be offering anything to the discussion, but on the other hand Leeming had previously in his Army life encountered the syndrome of men who were physically very strong but mentally reticent. Jakova was probably an interior person who would find himself forced by others into the role of leader simply because of his physical appearance of strength. Leeming wondered about that. Jakova didn't seem too sure of himself and yet it sounded like he was well used to giving orders. The trick of getting the maximum out of the man would be to convert him to taking orders. Leeming's mind shifted tack. "Why isn't the general here? Is all lay-out on this project processed from you?"

Buckman shrugged. "The general gets to hang out. This is an Army project. If something goes wrong, not one, but the whole hierarchy carry it."

"When do we go?"

Buckman looked to the other man. "On Spiro's nod. I guess about a week from now, maybe less."

"Tell me the mechanics. How we enter the country. What we do to locate Dhoc."

Buckman pursed his lips as if the plans were still unmade, though Leeming knew that he and the general must have gone over the precise details many times. "Perhaps within forty-eight hours, Meyer flies Spiro into Albania, landing in the mountains twenty miles north of Tiranha near a village called Kruje, ten miles from the coast. Next Spiro recruits his team and brings it back to the landing area. Meanwhile Meyer's returned for you and equipment. We have W/T contact with Spiro. We get his signal. You and Meyer go for Albania . . ."

Leeming was looking again at Jakova. The Albanian was pacing Buckman's words with nods. He seemed relaxed but alert. "You're going to have to give me time to think about this," Leeming told Buckman. "But first—what do you mean we locate Dhoc inside Albania through a certain person who knows where he is? What person? Who would have that information?"

Buckman stalled for a second but it was simply to

marshal a reply. "You have to hear me out fully. It's a wild scheme, the wildest the general ever thought up. But we think it's go. It'll work . . ."

Buckman talked for fifteen minutes and Leeming didn't interrupt. Jakova sat silent, sipping his wine. He'd obviously heard the outline. It was a simple concept. Leeming thought it could work. But he also knew that if any of its half-dozen components collapsed, he and the man sitting across the table from him would not get out of Albania alive.

16

LEEMING TOOK A CAB through the first fingerings of
dusk to the apartment block in the rue de Duras. He
stopped the driver outside the forecourt of the block.
There had not been a single word in the papers about
Caswell's murder, so she would know nothing. He had
not worked it all out, but he felt he owed it to Caswell,
that she be told the lieutenant had not simply run off
without a word.

He walked into the forecourt, crossed the cobbles
and reached the short flight of steps to her apartment.
There was a long pause after he rang the bell, and he
had begun to think that she was out. Then he heard a
security bolt snap back and she was standing there.

He suddenly realized that perhaps she wouldn't rec-
ognize him, that he might have to stumble out a rein-
troduction.

But she said, "John Leeming," and took his hand.
"Today is my butler's holiday. I'm alone. Come in and
give me your coat."

He stepped into the hall, took off his coat and looked
at her, really looked at her for the first time. Her expression seemed contained, indeterminate.

"And where is Stephen?" she asked finally.

There was a moment's pause. He sought for some
opening line that would soften the blow. The pause
lasted a little too long. He saw her face begin to fall and
her mouth tighten.

"Something has happened to him, yes?"

He nodded slowly. Somehow she knew, but she made it a question. "Is he dead?" The words were so soft that he at first didn't understand. He was surprised she had arrived so quickly at the query.

"Yes," he said.

She was standing still. Now her eyes slowly filled with tears and her shoulders lifted in little jerking motions. For some seconds she cried silently. Then she turned and moved across the hall through the narrow door into the sitting room where she sat down in an armchair that faced out of the window. "The last time, he told me we would spend next winter in America." Her voice seemed distant. "He described a place that he goes to—Sun Valley—skiing. He said he was quite a skier. He told me he was clever at everything. I believe he was. How was he not clever enough to stay alive?"

"Do you want to know how it happened?" Leeming had decided not to tell her the truth. He had prepared a story that Caswell had died in a light plane accident on a secret mission, and that the State Department had stopped details from reaching the press.

"He's dead. What does it matter?"

"He died for his country."

She turned her sad eyes on him and repeated, "It's irrelevant."

Leeming studied the view of her empty backyard, the high walls of the old apartment blocks facing hers, a tapestry of cement and gray brick, of kitchen products on ledges and washing seen through windows, and lights switching on as the day dimmed. "Perhaps a drink might help. Can I get you a brandy?"

"No," she said positively, her eyes concentrating on the walls outside as if she'd seen something. The silence grew. He could see the grip of her fingers tightening on the arms of the chair. Then, at the end of perhaps a minute, he saw some of the tension go out of her hands.

She stood up. She took his hand, and spoke quietly. "I appreciate that you came to tell me this. It's an ugly thing to have to be the conveyor of such horrible news. I know you could have avoided doing it—and Stephen and I were not your business. But you came here because you are an honorable man. I thank you." She started to steer him across the room toward the hall. "Some people need company to share the burden of their grief. Others like me, prefer to be alone. You understand?"

He nodded.

She led him into the hall and opened the front door. "I would like to see you again. Is that possible?"

"Yes," he said gently. "I'll phone you in a few days."

"Please remember."

He went down the steps into the courtyard. He was aware that she hadn't closed the door, had watched him as he walked across the courtyard and turned right into rue de Duras.

17

HE HAD BEEN HEAVILY dressed for the rock face but somehow he was cold. It was midday, no sun to be seen in the bleached denim-colored sky. The wind was sharp across the flat acres of the airfield at Melun. Buckman, Meyer and Jakova were unloading equipment from a jeep onto a trestle table. In the background, parked in the shade of a large double hangar that must have housed most of the props of the little airport, was the Feiseler. Next to the Feiseler the Breguet 401 that had brought him back from Provence.

Leeming had asked Jakova some general questions about Albania to pass the time while the boxes were being unloaded. Jakova was answering carefully, as if he wanted to be sure the American understood.

"We're the most fiercely independent people in Europe. We've a history of battles and bloodshed longer than any other nation. We fight all the time, our invaders, and each other. We invented the vendetta, you know. People think the vendetta is Sicilian. The idea of a Code of Honor started in my country. Everyone has an enemy. Mine is the Hoxha regime. Many think like me—many more do not. Communism in Albania got rid of a monster called King Zog, fed and clothed the poor people and the old people. These ones will sacrifice their lives to keep this creed. If these people find you they will betray you. But people like me say yes, communism has trained doctors, midwives, opened schools—but how many have died or disappeared? Why are so many in jail? Hoxha's government has terrorized us since 1945. It's now the oldest dictatorship in Europe. It has taken from the people the few things that were left over after the Nazis destroyed our country. They have left us little but our pride. Try to understand that."

"I'll try."

Leeming had come away from the Paris meetings having made no progress in penetrating Jakova's mind. All he had were surface impressions—the strong well-dressed man with a peasant's feeding habits. Jakova ate very untidily, chewing with mouth half open, and spilling food off his plate in his haste to demolish it. The performance had been particularly noticeable at two rendezvous in expensive restaurants. After the second Paris meeting, Buckman had described Jakova as a Balkan Moshe Dayan without the eyepatch. Leeming didn't think that was accurate, in fact he had come to a speculative conclusion that the man might be an Albanian variation on himself—a sort of professional soldier-adventurer gone wrong. Leeming's main area of worry was not being able to get a positive insight into Jakova's fundamental motives. He had listened now to quite a lot of talk from the Albanian but still could not decide in his own heart whether the man really was interested in this operation as a patriot, or whether he was in it for other reasons so far undisclosed.

Meyer had started to open the boxes. The first contained the Siamese Mauser Caswell had practiced with at the *baigneuse* on the Seine.

Leeming asked for the Mauser, tested the bolt action, broke it open, looked along the twin barrels. Someone had cleaned the gun since its use on the Seine. He passed the old weapon on to Jakova, who eyed it cautiously. Buckman saw the man's expression and explained. "Siamese Mauser. We understand a popular gun in your country. When they check the ballistics of the assassin bullet your police will hopefully think the killing is of native inspiration."

Jakova shrugged. He didn't know whether he agreed or disagreed with that.

Meyer had now opened a wooden case containing a Japanese-manufactured long-wave radio transmitter. Buckman explained that the instrument had a special directional transmitting aerial that could bounce the transmit beam off a distant object and confuse any attempt to locate the source of the transmitter.

They stood in the cold wind and discussed the radio for a few minutes. Buckman gave his final verdict— he'd tried it out earlier. It was a complicated piece of electronics but simple to operate.

Next came the guns. Buckman opened a fiberglass crate containing six machine pistols and bullet packs. "Just had a memo on those." He pronounced it "meemo." "These are brand new ordnance. They're M40 calibers, totally new out of Remington. Removable stock, can be used as a pistol. Removable pistol grip, can be used as a rifle." He took one of the short-barreled rifles out of the crate and demonstrated, sliding the rifle butt off the weapon from its friction seating, and then pulling back and snapping off the pistol butt. What was left was a barrel-tube and a two-inch-diameter back block. "You can stick this down the arm of your jacket."

The next crate contained books. There were three copies of each. Leeming glanced at the titles. K. Frasheri, "The History of Albania." Then typed translations, on Pentagon file-marked paper, of something titled *"Forschungen zur Albanishen Frühgeschichte"* by G. Stadmuller. An American publication, "Albania," edited by J. Sadeusz, another—"Albania and the Sino-Soviet Rift" by W. E. Griffith. Buckman shrugged his shoulders, a gesture of doubt at the point of the reading.

"I prefer reading maps," he told Buckman.

"The general particularly wants you to read some books. The different customs and mores. Spiro agrees."

Leeming gave a slow nod. He was beginning to wonder if in fact the general existed. He hadn't seen the man for ten days and was getting more uncomfortable working on a major initiative guided by through-put from subordinates.

The next package contained an Asahi 20X monocular and a Pentax K2 camera.

"The general wants holiday. photos." Buckman handed the camera to Leeming. Leeming began to check it over.

"Now the medic box, inside which, this little bag of tricks. Four pills of a new hallucinogenic coded Senibral." Buckman had opened up a red plastic First Aid box, and taken out from among the band-aids and bandages an unmarked small clear plastic container. The others could see the four large white pills in the phial. "We'll go into the precise data on Senibral later. Briefly the thing works as a memory block. The pill is administered and for five to seven days after, the patient has total memory failure, knows not who he is, where he's been, what he's done." Buckman put the pills back in the box and moved on to the next package—a canvas tool-roll.

Leeming studied the twenty heavy chrome steel tools—screwdrivers, wrenches, wire cutters—and shrugged. "Look," he said, "if I have the say, we travel light. I don't think we're going to need First Aid boxes, books and wire cutters."

"Tell the general," Buckman advised sharply. "I didn't organize this."

The next package was the largest. It contained climbing equipment, clothes, blankets, nylon rope, hammers, pitons, two pairs of boots, exposure foil, hard rations and several unidentifiable plastic packages.

Leeming had started in the morning confronting a three-hundred-foot rock face in Les Baux-en-Provence. He'd been picked up at the hotel at six A.M. and driven to Neuilly. A French Air Force Breguet was waiting, props turning over, to fly him the hundred and fifty miles to Les Baux, a pre-Roman town knifing up from the high flat plateau of Provence. Outside the town were some of the best-aged lime and sandstone rock climbs in France. At ten in the morning, fully kitted and freezing in the high wind chasing across the plateau, and following a French alpine instructor, he started up the face of the rock. The three-hundred-foot climb took two hours. He reached the narrow-angled top of the rock and sat down, exhausted, fingernails broken, fingers freezing, and his back, arm and leg muscles all signaling agony. He hadn't climbed a rock face in four years but at the top the instructor had pronounced *"Bon!"* and Leeming knew he meant it.

The descent took an hour and a quarter. Leeming arrived on flat earth with his confidence still intact, although he was concerned by his lack of physical reserves. He was not as fit as he thought he was. He wondered if he should tell the general about that. At the bottom of the rock face at Les Baux he decided he would not, a decision he was to regret very shortly.

Back at the airport at Melun, Leeming checked over the climbing equipment, all by Pegler, the leading German manufacturers. There was sufficient gear for moderate climbs without absailing overhangs, or anything else too elaborate.

Buckman opened the next hinged-top wooden crate. Leeming saw the dozen vari-sized tin cans of Dow gelignite, akracord and other pencil detonators.

"What weight?" Leeming asked.

"The jello is twenty pounds," Buckman said.

"What possible use would we have for twenty pounds of gelignite?" he asked flatly.

Buckman decided not to argue about it. "Whatever you want. Now what about some firepower. An M79?"

Leeming hesitated. There were two versions of the M79 grenade-launcher, one a self-contained rifle-type weapon with stock—the other, with the same designation, was designed to attach to the U.S. M16 rifle. "Let me think about it." He was staring across the flat acres of the airfield. A fighter was approaching, an F-100 Sabre. The others hadn't yet spotted the U.S. markings.

"So how much of this stuff do we pack to ship on the Feiseler?" Buckman wanted to know.

"I'll think about it."

"How long d'you reckon you've got to think about it?" Buckman's voice was getting testy.

"As long as it takes," Leeming said heavily.

For the next minute conversation was impossible as the piggyback twin jet engines of the Sabre screamed their protests at taxiing and shutdown. The pilot had spotted the group by the jeep and hauled the big fighter down the S-bends of the runway apron lanes to bring the aircraft to within fifty feet of them. The hydraulics pushed the canopy up and Leeming saw the man in the tandem position stand up behind the pilot. It was General Mackerras.

He was on his way to Rome, a NATO meeting. That's what he told them a minute after the nods and introductions. He had not met Jakova before. He exchanged a few noncommittal phrases with the Albanian, Meyer and Buckman, then led Leeming apart. He opened by saying that he had come to ask Leeming, confidentially, a couple of questions. How did the rock face go? What really was his verdict on the mission? Did he have any doubts at all?

Leeming gazed at the concentration on Mackerras' face as they strolled across the sparse winter grass. The man seemed distant and less precise than usual, a softer version of the SHAPE Headquarters general.

"Colonel, I want you to be sure about this mission. We've already had elements of the unexpected. There was a spy, presumably, in the Paris Vietnamese community, who pointed Van Dhoc at the lieutenant. That certainly came out of left field. Now I talk your language, and you add up to me, so I want to warn you there's a certain layering in this project. There are things about it I can't explain. But I promise you, stay on your toes and you've got all you need to carry it through to a successful conclusion."

"What are you saying?" Leeming asked gently.

The general paused, maybe trying to think of subtler ways to state his answer, then his lips pursed like he hadn't found one. "On this mission watch Buckman. If you have any worries about any areas communicate direct with me, not Buckman. And don't ever tell a living soul I gave you this order."

18

HE WAS GIVEN A few days to chew that over. It was probably sound advice about Buckman, but he'd already taken it by himself. He had been trusting no one. And if it came to writing out a list of names of people not to trust, highest on the list would be the general's.

Over the next four days he had three more meetings with Buckman and Jakova. The discussions ranged from fine detail to the vaguest generalities. There was too much in the plans which was unknowable and incalculable, but somehow Leeming wasn't worried. There was a distinct objective and a tolerable number of alternatives to achieve it. It was down now to honing the right state of mind, the will, and the energy.

He believed for no good reason that Buckman or anyone had hinted at, that the mission would still take ten days to a fortnight to the go-ahead. Five days after Melun, Buckman phoned him at ten A.M. to say that Meyer and Jakova would be on the Feiseler at 2300 hours and heading for Albania. The general's orders, subject to four-hourly review, were that Leeming's ETD would be six days from now, and meanwhile he could do what he wanted, provided he remained in the Paris environs.

He put down the phone more surprised than angry. The mission had commenced without his knowledge—a phone call after the event—then he shrugged it off. He had six days and plenty to do. Read the books, study the maps, work on contingency routes out of the country in the event that things went wrong. In the hands of these people he could calculate that he would have to back up everything with a contingency alternative.

All morning he studied the books and maps. Before lunch he phoned Lara. He hadn't seen her since three evenings ago, when he'd told her about the death of Caswell.

She seemed pleased to get his call. He said, "Come to Allard's. I feel like the kind of too much, too long lunch that'll ruin the rest of the day. How about you?"

She had not made any plans and she would like him to come first to the apartment for a drink perhaps.

He took a cab to the rue de Duras. He noticed he was being followed. There was a large man with horn rims in a small Peugeot 304 that kept a precise fifty yards between the Peugeot and his cab. He presumed that as he was now on alert for the operation, Mackerras's office would have ordered a routine surveillance to know his movements if they needed to get hold of him fast. And generally to keep an eye on him. There were two men in Albania on a mission whose success depended on his eventual arrival there. On the surface it was an obvious precaution.

She met him at the door. He'd wondered how she'd look, how she'd react to seeing him again. How she'd adjusted to the loss of Caswell, if she had. She seemed pale, a little reserved, but she took him by the arm as they moved into the sitting room. "I've thought about it," she said. "I want to know how Stephen died. Before you say anything, I will pour a cognac for myself. Would you like one?"

"Yes."

She went across to the rolltop Louis Quinze escritoire which served as the bar. She started to pour the drinks. "Tell me how it happened?"

"He was here to complete a military mission. I can't give details of that. Several days ago he flew from Paris to Les Baux-en-Provence. He and a pilot got into a mountain rescue plane. They were trying to land on a bridge, an aqueduct. The plane didn't make the aqueduct. It hit the mountainside. They were both killed instantaneously."

She handed him the brandy. Her eyes were studying him. She pondered the problem a moment and then said quietly, "You're lying to me. Why?"

"That's the truth."

"I ask a question but I know the answer. You lie because you want to protect me from the truth."

"No."

"You're a kind man." She took his hand and held it. "You are sympathetic. You must have experienced a lot of grief in your life."

He began to say something, thought better of it.

"Go on," she said.

"Lara, I've thought a lot about you, and I care for you." He felt that sounded lame, but he couldn't think of a way to word it more profoundly. "I want to see more of you. I want to stay here tonight."

"I hope you will," she said quietly.

"I've little to offer you. I'm on the same project, with the same risks Caswell took."

She was listening, but not processing the words to work out a decision. She'd already made it. "It's all right." She took both his hands and squeezed them. "Now let's go out."

Chez Allard was crammed to the doors with too many diners, tables, and waiters, scurrying fast around the pine and sawdust floor. The noise level was high. Many of the clientele in their expensive clothes with their svelte secretaries seemed to know each other. This was a rich man's restaurant disguised as a *routier*. Leeming had called for reservations at eleven A.M. His table was ready. He wondered about the big man with the horn rims in the small Peugeot. He guessed correctly that it would be easier for the man to get into the Kremlin than Allard at lunchtime without a booking. He and Lara had hardly sat down when the man came in. He'd removed his glasses, but it was the Peugeot man, and he couldn't get a table and was politely evicted.

They talked, questioning each other very gently, probing personal histories. He said little but generalities. He spoke about the outline of his life, dates of birth, marriage, Army, illness. She told him more of feelings than events. Born in Poland of a French mother, Polish father, both died in the war. Raised by an aunt who brought her to Paris. Lara was fifteen when the aunt died. She'd been involved with a dozen men, then met Franjou. She'd been lucky in some ways—for the last six years the man had financed her enough for a good life with, admittedly, nothing over to save. But his demands had been small. He was always jealous but she believed he had other mistresses and was equally jealous with them. He had not made a sexual demand on her now for nearly a year. It was dinner once or twice a week, and by the end of the meal he was either too tired or drunk. Lately he had been drinking more.

"What does he drink?"

"Wine."

"What kind of wine?"

"Modest wine. Corton Marachaudes '71 is his latest. I also like it."

"Can we get it here?"

"Possibly. And if as you said you want a too long lunch, I recommend it."

An hour went by and a meal of terrine, steaks, and one and a half bottles of Corton. They lost the impetus to order dessert and had coffee. The doors were constantly opening to release the clientele to their chauffeurs and offices. The restaurant was emptying.

The man in the Peugeot was parked directly across from the restaurant, as dutifully close as a chauffeur in a car.

Leeming, mildly drunk, asked Lara to excuse him one minute, got up, walked to the main door of the restaurant and out into the street.

Across the street the man studied his approach.

Leeming started across the street, heard the clunk and whirr of the Peugeot starter, and then the engine caught. He waved to the man to wait. The man hesitated. He reached the car. "We're here another half-hour. You get some eats. Then back to rue de Duras."

The man was suddenly revving the engine, slamming in the clutch, and the Peugeot was off down the rue Saint-André-des-Arts, back end slewing and wriggling with acceleration.

Leeming shrugged and returned to the restaurant.

They returned to her apartment. Lara disappeared into a tiny kitchen saying she would make more coffee. She came back a few minutes later with a silver tray with two cups and a glass percolator on it. She crossed the sitting room. He was sitting on an armchair. She moved into a bedroom, reappeared a moment later and stood in the doorway.

He got out of his chair and followed her into the bedroom.

She was standing by the bed, her expression uncertain.

He went up to her and held her gently. "I won't hurry you into this," he said.

"No. I want to."

They undressed silently, and got into bed. She wanted no preliminaries, as if nervous that if there was any delay she might change her mind. But once he had started to make love to her she slowed him. It took a long time, and then suddenly, almost unexpectedly, she climaxed, and he followed, and it was over and he moved off her and immediately she went into an exhausted deep-reaching sleep. She slept for two hours while he smoked several cigarettes. Finally she stirred. "What time is it?"

He checked his watch. "Five."

"Can you stay with me all night?"

"I have to make a phone call."

She nodded.

He got out of bed, sat down naked on a large pink velvet chair, and lifted the phone from the bedside table onto his knees. He called Mackerras's office and got through to the secretary. "I'm here until say 0800 tomorrow. 09.94.97. Check?"

The secretary repeated the phone number.

"Pass that to the guy who's gumshoeing outside. If he's surveillance, I don't like it. If he's security, I don't need it."

The secretary must have had instructions to tap the general's extension—maybe a phone loudspeaker box on the general's desk, in the event of certain calls.

Leeming heard the general's voice. "Mackerras here. What's your problem?"

"There's a man outside on follow-through. I don't know whether it's surveillance or protection but I don't need it. It's not important, but that's how I feel."

"He'll be removed," the general replied. "You appreciate you're still on four-hour stand-by? Or less if we get a weather-break situation."

"Yes, General."

Leeming rang off.

Mackerras stayed on the line till his secretary came on. "Harriet, get Buckman at the Services Club."

A moment later he was talking to Buckman. "Leeming's spotted a surveillance party on the hoof. Phone me."

Buckman returned the general's call about an hour and a half later. His voice was more exasperated than angry. "Subject about six-foot, fat, horn-rimmed glasses, Peugeot 304—plates false. He's not G2. He's not one of ours."

The silence from the general's end of the phone was more expressive than an outburst of blasphemy.

Buckman took the twenty-second pause as the general thought it out, then broke the silence. "What are we going to do about it, General?" His words were terse.

"Our man's in Albania putting it together. Colonel

Leeming's about to climb into that Feiseler. What d'you mean, what are we going to do about it? It's too late to do anything about it, it's just too fucking late, Buckman. . . ."

19

THE DRONE FROM THE engine was lulling. Meyer had given him a set of headphones, shot his plug into an appropriate jack beneath his feet, and the worst of the engine noise was replaced by the American pilot's vague commentary on speed, direction, weather and map references. Meyer was doing his own navigation. He never faltered from the first fix. The Feiseler, slicing through the low Adriatic clouds, never once had a major navigational correction.

Above, seen in gaps in the clouds, a quarter moon tried to light the pitch sky, a candle in a coal mine. A few rays did get through. There was a just visible surface on the plate-black glass of sea. And maybe a ten-mile visibility. Leeming didn't know, couldn't calculate visibility distances. On the east turn over Bari and the last reroute for the one-hundred-and-ten-mile Adriatic crossing to the Albanian coastline, Meyer had suddenly pushed the Feiseler down hard to a five-hundred-foot ceiling, and given Leeming plenty to speculate about on the subject of safety margins. The tach indicated a speed of less than a hundred miles per hour—Meyer had mentioned that the last part of the journey would be at extreme low altitude, the engine running at one-third revs for quietness. Leeming realized any kind of high frontal gust at this speed could be fatal.

At Ancona, as dusk fell and Meyer headed down the Italian coastline, he dropped the speed still further. "At knots one hundred, any Albanian radar will hardly note us on the Italian side—we look like a weekend Cessna trainer. Once we change course at Bari though, we gotta get down and under that radar, and dead slow, no heat-scan monitor tripping the U-V of our engine heat." He had said approaching Ancona, "Florence below there to the left. Most wonderful city in the world. Know it?"

Leeming shook his head.

"Go there one day."

Leeming wondered at the edge on Meyer's voice, but couldn't work out whether it was due to the stress of concentration, or worry.

"How did the first flight go?" Leeming asked. He'd mentioned Jakova and the first journey to Meyer at Melun, but had only gotten some generalizations.

Meyer must have heard the question, but hesitated for a moment. Then he said, "It's a bum landing site. It's a rock slab, maybe eighty feet long, walled in by other rocks. Torch-lighted—that's all they got. When we hit that rock you grab everything you hold dear. When we get down—if we get down—you'll realize why they hired me. I gotta be crazy."

Leeming absorbed that without comment.

"See there?" Meyer pointed.

He looked out. He could see nothing in the black drapes of night. Then he saw a pinprick of light, maybe a dozen miles away. "Ship?"

"The Durres lightship. We are now inside Albanian territorial waters. Means nothing unless you're employed by G2. Then it means if they grab you, you get shot."

No clear images now as Meyer banked gently away from the lightship and headed toward the coast, identified by vague mountain shadow and moonlight on water breaking over the rockline. The engine cut again. Leeming's eyes studied the blue-lighted rev-counter in the darkened cabin. The revs were pounding now at 600, the plane feathering its way in on a gentle descent over the last of the sea to the coast. An inshore breeze caught the Feiseler, giving it lift, but the lack of revs had the plane shaking, the old engine losing the smoothness that came from operational revs.

Three miles away to the south the crocheted lights of the port of Durres, the minute white string dots of streetlights ran up and down the black velvet shape of the town. Leeming saw the vague outline of a wide-metalled road slipping by below, no lights or traffic moving on it.

"Get those grab-handles, hold tight," Meyer ordered, but didn't wait. He banked the Feiseler in a sudden change of direction to place the plane running due north up the coast. Then he put on the revs. The engine clattered up the noise scale to reach four thousand cruising peak. "If we're seen on radar now they'll guess we're an internal flight." He shrugged. "That's the hope." Then he was checking his wide-dialed Patek Phillipe. "Minus four minutes to ETA. Hold again. Check harness. Final approach. Look for maybe a half-dozen torchlights, over there," he pointed, "the mountains."

Leeming saw them first. A half-dozen, maybe more, pinpricks of light moving back and forth, marking out the perimeters of a rough octagonal shape in the darkness below.

Meyer banked the craft again, studying out of the side windows, calculating a judgment that would put them safely down on the weathered surface of a bumpy slab of rock in the almost pitch dark. Leeming was watching Meyer's face in the blue up-lighting from the instruments. The man seemed less worried now, perhaps because he had his mind full of the mechanical problems of the landing. He pulled the plane creaking around on a tight locus, actuated spoilers, and dropped the nose toward the torches and the touchdown.

Ten seconds of nightmare as the craft touched, bounced, braked, slewed and hurled Leeming forward on his seat with enough force to put his head through the windscreen had not the harness arrested his body with a bone-thumping jar. The plane stopped, engine turning over in splutters of preignition, then finally halting with a couple of backfires. He felt blood on his lips. He had bitten his tongue. He had forgotten that he should have treated this as a para-drop—positioned tongue down pressing hard against the back of lower front teeth. He swallowed the salt taste and looked at Meyer. Meyer had switched on the cabin lights, looked out at the faces first, a vague wave to the only familiar one, Jakova, and then he turned to Leeming. "Okay?"

Leeming nodded.

"Smile, Colonel. Your day is over. I have yet to fly this canary off this real estate."

Someone from the Jakova party was opening the port exit door from the outside. Meyer had taken a half bottle of Camus brandy from a store slot in the cabin wall on his right side. He spun off the cap and took a swig. He offered it to Leeming.

Leeming shook his head. "You'll make it," he said. "Thanks for the ride."

"I didn't get told what brings you here. Whatever it is, I wish you success."

"Thanks again."

Meyer helped with the unloading. The bullion came first. Two small boxes containing quarter-kilo bars, $15,000 worth. It represented half the payment to the group, the other half would be delivered by Meyer on the completion of the job. Leeming had noticed that since his original conversation with Buckman, the purpose of the gold payment had shifted from a lump sum paid to the group to buy goods to fight its enemy, to individual payments to each member of the group. However this initial sum of $15,000 seemed precious little to help buy their loyalties. He could remember a North Vietnamese field contact who used to pick up nearly $40,000 every month when he walked into Leeming's Special Forces Camp with a letter containing just one page of the North's troop movements.

How many were there in the dark? No time to stop, ask for a torch, probe the darkness. At first he thought it was six men including Jakova. Then he saw another man, tall and dark-skinned, with Turkish-curled mustache and deep hard eyes. Then he thought he saw, standing above the entrance to a cave, a girl.

They were urgently moving the equipment from the Feiseler up the slab of rock to a cave. Leeming wondered at their haste. Dawn was two hours away. Maybe they wanted to get the Feiseler back in the air, give Meyer a long stride to safety before daybreak. Or maybe this group was already being hunted, and any extended halt in one place was a danger.

He had twenty after two on his watch when the plane was finally unloaded and its tail lifted by four of the strongest men and carried around in a semicircle to face it out to sea again. When the engine started it sounded like the whole mountain range was caving in as every decibel echoed off the noise-bouncing rock. "They'll hear this in Durres, in Tiranha," Leeming said to himself. But suddenly the Feiseler peaked its revs, rolled forward and then seemed to jump in the air and was gone.

"I go to the cave now, Colonel. We discuss the gold. Who gets how much." Jakova was standing by Leeming's elbow. "You wait just outside. There will be rows of course. That's usual. I hope nothing else."

Leeming crossed to a rock, sat down on it and stared out to sea in the direction that Meyer and the plane had taken. Dawn burst in a red aurora behind the needle peaks and high valleys between the mountains. He saw gulls wheel inland from the stark gray plate of empty sea—maybe a storm offing, or the normal journey of these parasites inland to check the rocks for the small animal corpses of another night of nature's deaths. Around him it looked like the surface of the moon. Miles of old and deep-fissured volcanic rock untouched by vegetation. Looking in any direction he could see at least five miles of this strange landscape. So the first objective must be to walk, clamber, jump and climb a way out of this.

If the mission started at all. Inside the cave there were nine of them and one was a girl. They had been shouting at each other for two hours in hard, harsh voices. Voices that would worry any man not used to the violence of language of frontline assault troops in Vietnam. But in Vietnam they'd screamed at each other for a million reasons but none to do with the wages to be paid to search and destroy.

At one point Leeming got up and walked into the cave. "What's happening for God's sake?"

"We are near to settling."

"Get it wrapped up. Later I want an explanation— why we had to start off with this goddam idiocy."

"This is the way of business in Albania."

"I don't care for it."

Jakova started to bristle. "This is the way it is done, Colonel."

With a sour expression Jakova went back inside the cave. Leeming returned to his small rock perch, sat down and awaited daylight.

They moved out at five o'clock, clattering over the rocks, stepping, sliding across the gulleys, the loose scree, heading south for the plain which rolled out of the mountain range and down toward the sprawl of the capital, Tiranha, twenty miles away. As the group clambered slowly over the tip of one huge crevasse, Leeming spotted in the Asahi monocular to the east and five miles away a village perched on the top of a huge rock, sheer drops on all sides, a single staircase up to it cut out of the side of the rock. It looked stark and peaceful in the morning light. He remembered Jakova saying at one of the meetings, "The country is beautiful. Magnificent mountains, picturesque villages, brilliant architecture, golden mosques, splendid churches, breathtaking castles, color everywhere, from the poppy fields to the clothes of the people—vivid head scarves, striped aprons, embroidered jackets. But remember one thing. My people, the Albanians, live in this most beautiful country, but are the wildest, most suspicious, murderous people in the world."

Leeming continued down the crevasse. Daylight had shown the faces of these men. Four of them appeared Greek or Turkish. The others were probably indigenous, one distinctly Italian-looking, long groomed black hair, long nose and fingers, and a nervous look, and, as if to suggest a further Italian connection, he carried a Beretta .380 with a fitted short stock on a piece of thick string looped through the trigger guard. When Leeming first saw this, he wanted to check with Jakova that the Beretta's magazine was empty—he'd seen enough accidents with guns, but on closer inspection he decided it was not likely this character would make a mistake with any gun. He looked like a professional assassin.

They had started down the rock face in single file. Within minutes the going had gotten harder. The men broke into three groups, each group finding its own route, but staying within shouting distance of each other. If the Feiseler's approach had been picked up by radar or U-V heat skan, the authorities would have plenty of time. They would know that anyone who landed in the mountains at night would wait for daylight before coming down, and that the journey across the miles of crevasses would take a morning.

After the first half-mile Leeming realized that he was tiring quickly. They had worked their way down the rock face, heading, possibly because it was some form of landmark, toward a group of fir trees. Leeming walked ahead of the others to the edge of the ledge where the trees perched.

He was staggered by what he saw. The mountain fell away in a series of precipitous steps down, maybe another two thousand feet, to a valley about half a mile away. Then a rise, another screen of sharp-edged pinnacles up to the high hill beyond. To the right beyond this hill, the fertile flow of green, the white-speck villages, and then more hills, but lower and farther apart—and then presumably a walk on flat ground would find a road leading to the capital.

But the valley below the ledge—there was no conceivable way that he could cross this in a matter of hours. He turned around and looked for Jakova.

"How long will this take?" Leeming indicated the half-mile sprawl of rocks and deep crevasses.

"Three hours," Jakova answered. "Why?"

"There's some easy route through it?"

"I'm sorry." Jakova shook his head. "We have to go straight across the tops."

"That's not possible in three hours."

Jakova looked puzzled. "Why?"

"The girl. These men. We're carrying equipment. You'd need a really experienced climber to cross these bluffs in three hours."

"Who d'you think these people are? How do you think I selected them? Two of the men are coaches at the Djati School—very famous climbers' school. The rest, like you, are all highly experienced climbers. This is nothing for them."

Leeming's heart sank as he looked back at the rolling waves of peaks and deep clefts. He had learned at the top of the rock face at Les Baux-en-Provence that the years had caught up with him. They moved down to the first sheer two-hundred-foot climb. He looked it over. It would require an absail up a rock funnel, back to one wall, feet pressed together, working the body up, tight rope work from above and below for the full drop of its sixty feet. Jakova went up first—a fly sprinting up a wall—effortless, textbook climbing, each handhold as precise as the beat of a conductor's baton. The others were silent, watching the man go up, studied interest on their faces. Obviously he had a reputation as a climber. The girl went next. She got her ropes tangled on a maneuver halfway up the face. There were shouts from below. *"Kudjes! Kudjes!"* Then her name: "Skendi." He studied her. Her body was thin-hipped, strong. She was wearing jeans, the trouser legs cut off just below her knees, and a blue shirt. She managed to spin herself free of the rope hitch and played the freed rope away from the run of pitons. She got near to the top and Jakova gave her one quick pull on the rope up the last six feet and she was standing on the summit, holding her sides, breathless. But her strength had not run out on the climb.

It was Leeming's turn. He had no problems till he

started up the beginning of the funnel. Halfway up the funnel he traversed out on the rope to look for handholds on the sheer face. He found some but they were sparse. He had pitons and a hammer. He started to hammer in his own piton hand-grips. He was aware of silence from above and below. They were all watching him. It was arguable that he was setting up an alternative possibility for anyone who, like himself, didn't care for the press-up method of scaling the funnel, but about seventy feet up he looked for the next crevasse in the rock where he could hit a piton in, and saw nothing. The rock above him was as flat and polished as a sheet of steel. Stuck fast on the side of the rock he faced his first real black doubt. He should have corrected Jakova's assumption that he was an experienced climber. Survive this climb and in the next hours how many more problems like this were going to confront him? He felt a pull on the safety rope and looked up. He could just see the top of Jakova's head twenty feet above.

"Pendulum. Traverse left. I'll hold. Get back in the funnel. There will be handholds inside the funnel."

Leeming slowly released his hold on the last piton and felt the rope cut into his waist as he placed his whole weight on it—Jakova was now carrying him. He pushed himself out from the wall, gave a kick and his body careened over to the left to the extent of the rope's travel past the funnel, and then started to swing back. His hand went out and he grabbed the edge of the funnel and pulled himself in. He looked round. Jakova was right. There were cracks and handholds. He got out his hammer and banged a piton in, anchored the rope, took a twenty-second rest to still the pounding of his heart, and began to climb. The next fifteen feet took ten minutes—the silence ominous from Jakova and the others. When he reached the top, Jakova gave him a helping hand for the last few feet. The girl did not look at him.

Half an hour was all it took to get the other men up the rock. Just enough time for Leeming to recover his strength, get up and set off for the next crevasse.

He stopped at the lip of the next crevasse and his

heart sank again. It was a hundred and fifty feet of gentle slope, but the climb out of it was higher and sheerer than the last funnel.

It could have happened to anyone, even Leeming himself. When they got to the bottom of the crevasse, Jakova, no doubt motivated by the thought that Leeming might get into trouble again, decided to make the climb simultaneously with two of the strongest-looking of the seven. Leeming guessed the man's calculation: if it came to the worst, three large men could pull him up the side of the crevasse. The calculation was not put into effect. The second man met with a minor accident halfway up the face. A piton banged in by Jakova had held for the first man. The second man had hardly grabbed it when it came away in his hands and his body dropped instantly fifteen feet. Jakova, on a ledge, had the safety line well anchored. A shouted conversation ensued, everyone joining in. The man finally was waving his left hand up so Jakova could see it. It was covered in blood. Leeming shouted up at Jakova. "What's happened?"

"His fingertips have lost their skin. He can't climb. We lower him."

Leeming thanked God for the accident that had saved him from failure and humiliation in the eyes of the group.

Jakova and the other man at the top of the climb slowly lowered the injured man to the bottom. Leeming saw the man's hand. The flesh of the fingertips had been torn away in protecting his head from the wall during the short fall. He found the First Aid box in the girl's backpack and offered her the Band-Aids to dress the man's finger wounds.

Jakova and the first man were back down within ten minutes. Jakova said, "Fuck," for Leeming's benefit, and then a string of Albanian obscenities. He sat down on a rock, took out a pack of cigarettes, didn't offer the pack around, and lit one.

"What happens?" Leeming asked.

"Because of this accident it will take us all day and into the night to go the long way around. Fuck," he said again. Then he shrugged it off, got up, threw the un-smoked cigarette away and set off down the defile.

20

JAKOVA WALKED THEM OUT onto the plain. It was nine in the evening. They made a weary crew, stumbling along in a darkness dimly lit by a quarter moon. The group was now spread out in single file over several hundred yards. Jakova led, the girl followed him, and then Leeming and the others. When they reached the Skoda truck there was a cheer. A journey that should have taken three hours had taken more than fourteen.

There was difficulty starting the truck. Jakova churned the starter which powered a series of gasps and explosions until finally the engine caught. The truck had box wood sides and a dirty green canvas canopy with tent flaps at the back. Leeming made a mental note that in the future he must check all items, especially transport, furnished by Jakova as the ancient vehicle shuddered out of the gas station and turned right onto the main road south into the capital.

They had been driving five minutes when Jakova, steering around a corner, suddenly slammed on the brakes. A mile below, at the bottom of the hill, there was a military roadblock. Leeming could count around a dozen khaki-colored Army trucks, at least a hundred soldiers spilled out in groups along a stretch of the road. They had halted and were minutely searching every truck and car coming from the north.

"So Meyer didn't get under the radar," Leeming said gently.

"It could be a routine search." Jakova's voice sounded worried.

"Whatever kind of a search we can't risk it."

"There was a turning to the right at the top of that last hill."

"Let's move."

Somehow the truck managed to make the climb up to the corner and the left turn into a narrow acacia-lined lane. The headlights were of hardly enough power to pick out the meanderings of this new route down through the screen of trees—there had been streetlamps on the main road.

"You know how to circle the roadblock to Tiranha?"

"It'll take a little time," Jakova said. "But we'll do it."

It took an hour and a half. It was around ten-thirty when they approached Tiranha down a suburban road from the northwest.

Leeming saw the first flowerings of workers' condominiums on the outskirts, tall blocks of modern apartments with exteriors painted in plain whitewash, like the houses in a Sienna hill village. The truck moved faster now on the newish roads through the suburbs, and then, coming over a crest of a hill, they were suddenly descending on Tiranha, its loose sprawl picked out by the patterns of streetlights, the town surrounded by the protective castellations of small hills, with the huge Mount Dajti looming up behind it.

"We go to the east of the city," Jakova said. "Stereo Cerrik, the thin-faced one, has a house near the Hunters Club. We stay there tonight."

"As soon as we get there I want to talk to these men."

"As soon as we arrive they'll want to go home to their families. We are doing nothing before the morning."

"I'll talk to them tonight." Leeming said it firmly. He must establish that he expected Jakova to follow orders.

Jakova shrugged his broad shoulders but did not dissent.

As the Skoda made its way to the center of the city, Leeming asked, "How come all this group are climbers?"

"In my country mountain climbers are usually enemies of the regime."

"Why?"

"Because they can get out. Compare our monstrous politics with other systems. Also climbers are the main source of black-market goods."

"Why don't you leave this place permanently?"

"The answer is simple. We're Albanians. Hoxha and his gangsters have stolen our country. One day we'll get it back." Jakova's gloomy voice somehow suggested a questionable conviction in what he was saying.

"Tell me about the girl."

Jakova's eyes left the road and he looked hard at Leeming. "Don't get interested in her. She's not for you."

Leeming eyed him coldly. "She's part of this group. Tell me who she is—why there's a girl in your group?"

Jakova braked the truck. A large pantechnicon was trying to back into a narrow parking space between two buildings. Then he said, "Her husband was a schoolteacher. He was found guilty of an invented treason at a secret trial. He was sent to jail two years ago. He died in jail one year ago. She says the *Shteti Policiza* murdered him. I warn you away from her because she now has this vendetta. The other men respect this and would be angry if they saw an outsider coming between her and her vendetta. You must learn we are a highly sensitive people."

Leeming wondered how far the evident passions and intransigencies of these people were going to either aid or complicate his plans.

The Hunters Club sat at the bottom of the highest of the capital's hills. Crowning the hill stood the palace built by King Zog, the last monarch of the country. The huge hundred-roomed edifice dominated the town. Cerrik's house was in a narrow street directly across from the wood-beamed Hunters Club. The house was white-

washed inside and out, clean, neat, with a low-ceilinged
sitting room containing fine carpets and sofas. An old
man rose to greet them as they entered, then hastened
from the room, after some discussion, to produce *café
turc*. He returned a minute later with a large silver pot.
He poured the small cups of the thick black coffee,
ferrying each one individually to its recipient, bowing
his head slightly before handing it over, the whole process conducted in silence.

Leeming found the sharp thick black coffee a good
antidote to the exhaustion of flying, climbing and
marching cross-country.

"I'll talk to them now," he told Jakova.

Jakova shrugged.

Leeming walked in among the men, held a hand up
for silence. "I'd like to introduce myself," he said. "My
name is Leeming."

Jakova came and stood by him and translated.
"Tungjat jeta, em emeni, Leeming. . . ."

He reckoned it shouldn't be difficult to explain. At
the meetings he and Buckman had had with Jakova in
Paris, it had all sounded straightforward, the orchestra-
tion of who did what, and how the Van Dhoc search
could serve a dual purpose. What Leeming needed to
know was that Jakova had made the ramifications clear
to the group, held nothing back, that these people knew
exactly what was planned, what they were up against,
and what was expected of them.

"I have come to your country to find a man. He is
Vietnamese. His name is Van Dhoc. He's hiding in Albania." He paused and listened while Jakova translated.
He watched their faces—all of them were studying Jakova, except the girl. The girl was looking directly at
him.

"We don't know where he's hiding. We're positive
there's one man who does. That man is Colonel General
Kellezi, chief of State Internal Security. As head of
State Internal Security, it's his department that would
have made the arrangements for Van Dhoc to come to
Albania and be accommodated here. All of you know

Kellezi. It's a hated name." He waited for Jakova to translate. The men were quieter now but their eyes, like the girl's, were beginning to shift to Leeming.

"Now, you are resistance fighters. The Hoxha regime has destroyed your country, put your families in jails or murdered them."

Jakova translated. The room was totally silent.

"Colonel General Kellezi is in many ways the man who makes it possible for the Hoxha regime to go on. Because of that, you people who are fighting for freedom must consider him your number-one target. He is also my target." Leeming paused and listened to the quiet drone of Jakova's words.

He went on. "I need Kellezi to tell me where to find Van Dhoc. You want Kellezi because he can tell you many things. Information about the workings of the regime, whether certain people who have disappeared—some of them cousins and brothers of yours—are dead or alive. And finally, when we have that information, we can both deal with him. I have brought guns and equipment. I believe it's possible, from what Spiro tells me, to kidnap this man, get information from him and deal with him. I made detailed plans in Paris. I'll need two days of research here to see if what I worked out is feasible. Thank you for listening to me. D'you have any questions?"

One of the men, a thick-set twenty-year-old with heavy black eyebrows, did have a question. Jakova translated: how, after they'd kidnapped the colonel general, did Leeming think he was going to make the man talk?

"I'm trained in methods of obtaining information from people. When we catch this man he'll tell us all we want to know."

This answer was received in silence.

Cerrick, whose house it was, now asked what plans Leeming had worked out in Paris.

Leeming answered and Jakova translated. "First we do our research. We must study Kellezi's movements. Then I'll give you my exact appraisal. I understand he has bodyguards. But I'm sure nine of us, properly organized, can handle them."

One of the older men suddenly spoke. Jakova turned to Leeming. "He says he will go home now to dispose of his gold in a hiding place. He will see us tomorrow."

All the others were suddenly finishing their coffee and standing up, or moving toward the door.

"Tell them to wait ten minutes while we discuss a few more points."

"Leeming, they are tired, and they are going."

"There are urgent matters to discuss," Leeming snapped, but he knew he'd lost the initiative.

"I bid them goodnight from you." Jakova turned and started shaking hands. "I will tell them to be here early in the morning."

The men filed past the metal-studded door, Jakova shook their hands and then they were gone. The girl finished her coffee and wandered out.

"Come and sit," Jakova said, as soon as the room was empty. He suddenly seemed expansive, as if he'd had to play a subdued role in front of the others. "It was a long day. You must be exhausted. For us it is easier, but you are not experienced in the rocks. Come and have more coffee in front of the fire."

Leeming allowed the man to take his elbow and steer him over to the sofa nearest the fire. "What time did you tell them to come back?"

"Around eight A.M."

"Are they reliable? Will they be here at eight?"

Jakova went over to the huge silver coffee pot. "They will turn up at eight. What I mean is that those who, having met you and listened to the plan, still do not think you are insane, will turn up at eight."

21

HE COULDN'T SLEEP. HE should have been exhausted by the journey down from the mountains, but he wasn't. It couldn't have been the strong *café turc*—coffee never kept him awake. It was his mind racing along, starting to marshal the sequence of decisions that he must begin making as soon as he got out of bed, and thinking back to random images of Paris, Buckman, Mackerras, and Lara in another bed with its pink coverlet in the apartment in rue de Duras. He felt as he tossed and turned a sudden need for her, and a realization that only by leaving Paris had he got her into perspective and that she was important to him. Meeting her was possibly the most important event that had happened in his private life for nearly a decade.

The night dragged its poor hold on him into the dawn. He lay there, frequently consulting his watch. Then about seven o'clock he heard noises, doors opening and closing in the house. He felt sure he smelled bread baking and then he did smell the pungent welcome of coffee.

He got out of bed, dressed, and went in search of the kitchen. He pushed open the door and halted in his tracks. She was standing in the center of the room, wearing a rough-woven skirt wrapped around kilt-style. He feet were bare on the brown tile floor. She was washing herself in a large gourd of water placed on the table. She was naked from the waist up. She was not using soap, just washing sleep away with warm water, caressing it down her face and neck and over her breasts.

He expected a reaction, but she just nodded to him, and splashed her face and neck again.

"*Tungjat jeta,*" she said. "*Urd heroni brinda.*"

He understood only the first part. It was, "Good morning." "*Tungjat jeta,* Skendi," he said.

She gave him a quick little smile, then took up some soap and carefully washed her neck and her firm beautiful breasts. He didn't see it as a provocation. The scene was perfectly natural. He had walked in, and she would finish her washing. She was pointing now to the door beyond. He wasn't sure what she was trying to convey. She took his arm, walked him over to the dresser, picked up a coffee cup, and directed him into the dining room. It was simply furnished with a pine table and six pine and rush chairs. In the middle of the table sat the huge silver coffeepot he'd seen last night, some earthenware plates, one containing lumps of brown bread, another an hors d'oeuvre of salami, goat cheese and sardines.

He ate some bread and drank the *café turc.* Five minutes later he heard the sound of the wash bowl being emptied into the sink. She came in wearing a white cotton shirt. She nodded to him again and poured herself some coffee.

A quarter of an hour later Jakova arrived. "I have been in Kunin since dawn. It's a suburb of large houses, high-position *narodnikis* and politicos. The Kellezi villa is maybe eight rooms, two floors, with a high wall around it. The entrance and exit are heavily guarded and other guards patrol the grounds. On the one hand it looks possible." Jakova's face was pensive. "On the other hand the house is a fortress." He had entered carrying a workman's tool bag which he now opened. "This thing is excellent," he said, bringing out the monocular. "I sat on the hill above the Kellezi villa. I could almost read the writing on his private papers."

"The villa's overlooked by a hill?" Leeming queried.

"We can sit on the hill, watch the comings and

goings, learn his routine." Jakova had poured a cup of coffee. He lifted it up and drank it back in a gulp. Then he took up a piece of black bread and stuffed it into his mouth and chewed, crumbs falling out of the corner of his mouth. "Come," he said to Leeming. "We begin work immediately."

He and Leeming and the girl walked out into the sunlight, up the narrow cobbled street two hundred yards to its top. Some of the men from yesterday's climb were waiting by two Skoda cars.

"I have obtained two automobiles," Jakova said. "To your American eyes they look old. For Albanian cars they are excellent. They have been serviced by an engineer, a good friend of mine. They will give no problems."

Leeming was pleased that Jakova had registered his admonitions about sound transport. "Where are the rest of the men?"

Jakova shrugged vaguely. "Only four are with us. Four and the girl."

"What d'you mean, four are with us?"

"I mean the others have decided they're not interested in your job."

Leeming felt his anger begin to rise. "They took the gold, thousands of dollars in gold."

"You've lost the gold, and them," Jakova said quietly.

"I didn't lose it. You chose them. You lost it. So what the hell are you going to do about it?"

They were now standing among the four men.

Jakova looked thoughtful. "Two out of seven have gone. Their disappearance will paradoxically double the determination of these others to succeed. An Albanian's pride is hurt when a foreigner is shown another Albanian is a coward. These men—Cerrik here, Pilo, Haziz and Dmitri—will now die to prove Albanians are not cowards."

"How do we replace the lost men?" Leeming demanded angrily.

"We don't. What has to be done can be done with the seven of us."

Leeming stopped himself. It was not the time to start a major row. "All right, give these people their orders."

Jakova sorted out the group into the two cars, and they drove off. Jakova turned to Leeming. "Everything will be fine, Leeming," he said.

Leeming said nothing, reserving his opinion. If Jakova couldn't get a functioning team together then he himself would have to pull out.

The Ministry of Internal Security, Tiranha, was a large building with a pillared façade. Italian-built during the Occupation, it had served virtually the same purpose then as now, thirty years later. Jakova parked the truck near the Via Muzeu, the street of museums, dominated by the House of Culture.

The four men and the girl had gone off to start the surveillance of the Kellezi villa. Leeming and Jakova had chosen to stake out Kellezi's Ministry. They got out of the truck and moved down Via Muzeu to a bus stop near the corner. It was just before midday. Leeming studied the building across the intersection, the porticoed entrance, the four floors, the small windows behind the important façade. There was a guard in civilian clothes standing just inside the front door, a submachine gun slung over his shoulder. In ten minutes a dozen people entered and left the building. Each was stopped by the guard and produced a security pass. Jakova anticipated Leeming's thoughts. "Two exits at the rear, not accessible to automobiles. He must enter or leave by the front."

"I see a place to park the truck," Leeming said.

A hundred and fifty yeads to the left of the bus stop, in a side street, there was a large building site. A group of men were preparing foundations with excavators and pile drivers. Various trucks stood around the outside.

They returned to the Skoda. Jakova drove down Via Muzeu and parked next to the building site. They now had a good view of the front of the Ministry.

It was more than an hour's wait. At one o'clock the

women factory workers appeared in their overalls and heavy wool coats. At one-twenty the guard inside the front door of the Ministry came down the steps and stood at the edge of the curb. A minute passed and then a chauffeur-driven Lada estate car came up the road. The guard walked back up the steps and inside. Seconds later he reappeared, this time preceding three men—the first two were guards, each carrying a carbine. The third was a tall man in a lightweight iron-gray suit exactly matching the color of his hair. He was about fifty, his face thin but his body slightly overweight.

"That's Kellezi," Jakova said, tight-lipped. He turned the key and started the engine. "Let's see where he goes for lunch."

Kellezi slid into the passenger seat of the Lada. The two men with carbines climbed inside and the car took off immediately. Jakova revved the engine and the truck started forward. The Lada headed into the heavy traffic. The chauffeur began using the horn, and the traffic opened up. Jakova followed through the opening. At the bottom of the street the Lada took a left turn and within ten minutes they were onto the beginnings of the wider roads leading to the suburbs and Kunin.

"He's heading for his villa," Jakova said. "And we're going to lose him." The Lada had picked up speed.

"Slow," Leeming commanded sharply.

"We'll lose him!"

"Slow!" There was something in Leeming's voice, and when Jakova turned to look at him, he saw the color had drained from the American's face. "We're being followed. . . ."

Jakova lifted his foot from the accelerator. Leeming's eyes were glued to the cracked mirror on the right front side. The car behind them was identical to Kellezi's—a chauffeur-driven Lada but with one armed guard riding in the back. It was the sight of the man next to him that had shocked Leeming. The tall sallow passenger was Van Dhoc.

"Left!" Leeming commanded, his voice cracking.

Jakova slowed the truck, made a leisured hand signal, braked and turned onto a poorly surfaced side street. Then he accelerated. Leeming watched his side mirror. Seconds later he saw the Lada with Van Dhoc in it cross the line of the mirror to continue following Kellezi's car.

"Pull up," Leeming ordered. He was trying to keep the anger out of his voice. He should have spotted the second Lada earlier. It had obviously commenced its journey from the same starting point as Kellezi.

"Van Dhoc," he told Jakova.

Jakova didn't seem to understand, and then he too reacted, dismayed that their quarry had been within yards of their grasp.

"Nothing we can do here with just one Smith and Wesson. Continue on to the villa."

Jakova started the engine, put the truck into a U-turn and headed back for the main road.

"If Van Dhoc isn't at the villa, do something for me," Leeming said.

"What?"

"Don't tell the others we saw him."

"Why?"

"I think it will screw morale if they hear we located our target and blew it."

"They would understand," Jakova said.

"We have to lead these people. They must respect us. We've done something which doesn't inspire respect."

Jakova shrugged as if the argument was irrelevant. "If you say so," he said flatly, still unable to keep the disappointment out of his voice.

They drove to Kunin. Jakova parked the truck half a mile away from the Kellezi villa, and they got out and walked to a lane lined with acacias which led up to some church ruins crowning a small hill. They were met by the four men and the girl. Skendi told them Kellezi's car had arrived ten minutes ago. They asked her if there had been any other cars. She said no.

The villa lay behind a fifteen-foot-high wall surrounded by well-groomed lawns. The view was slightly obscured by an old factory which Jakova said was a tobacco-drying plant. There were no telephone wires visible. Obviously the house would have telephones—therefore the precaution had been taken to put the wiring of these underground, so as not to be vulnerable to sabotage. Thought had obviously been given to security—and if this one thing had been done, what else? Leeming thought about the problem. The likeliest approach would probably be the simplest, breaking into the house at night and grabbing Kellezi at gunpoint. Jakova had said Kellezi lived with his child, a small boy. The wife had died during a second pregnancy. The man was now a fifty-year-old bachelor with a well-known appetite for young girls. He would be at home in bed most nights with one of them.

There were two small arched doorways in front and back of the exterior walls. Each had a sentry alongside it. In each of the sentry boxes an armed civil policeman was guarding the iron-grilled gates. Both gates were too narrow for a car to enter. Leeming decided that was also part of the careful security. A time bomb can be planted in a car or delivery van. So no entrance or exit for vehicles. This meant that anyone entering or leaving the villa would have to circumnavigate the dog or dogs. Leeming could see a giant brown German shepherd asleep on the ground near kennels to the left of the house.

As he studied the villa Jakova gave him thumbnail biographies of the four men sitting with the girl outside in the long grass. The youngest was called Haziz, Jakova said. He was just over twenty-one. Ethnically of Turkish origin, Haziz, like Cerrik, had first gotten into trouble with the state while a conscript in the Army. He'd put his signature on a petition complaining about the corruption of certain officers, and ended up in an Army jail for a year. He had a boyish face but hard eyes. His hair was cut short and oiled or pomaded flat. He was the best-looking of the four.

Stereo Cerrik was ten years older than Haziz, also of Turkish genealogy, but darker skinned, with a broader face and two small white scars on his right cheekbone.

On the climb yesterday it was he who carried the Beretta on a string around his neck. He looked like a man who thought things through carefully, then—having made a decision—stuck to it. Leeming felt Cerrik could be relied upon like a well-engineered piece of machinery.

The other two, Pilo and Dmitri, were cousins, Jakova said. Leeming had noticed on the march yesterday they kept close together. They were large men in their early thirties with low guttural voices. Their genealogy was an Italian-Balkan mix. Pilo's hair was blond, Dmitri's light brown. Pilo had the thinner face, Dmitri's was heavier and he carried the beginnings of a paunch.

Leeming thought about the four and realized he'd probably never succeed in getting to know them well. Nonetheless they did have some things in common. All their expressions were hard and cold.

Jakova started describing Kellezi's career. The man had been a minor politician when Hoxha first began transforming Albania from a totally illiterate, impoverished feudal society, whose few resources had just been savaged by the German-backed Italian occupation, into a high-literacy society where it was impossible to die of malnutrition or lack of medical care. Kellezi rapidly made a name for himself in Internal Security. His show trials became famous. The accused was usually a blameless figurehead. Kellezi's message was not that the personage was guilty, but that no one was innocent, everyone was vulnerable.

"Two things to remember about Kellezi," Jakova said. "He is the most hated man in the country and one of the most powerful. The first works in our favor—in a crisis some people will help us, perhaps. The second against us. When we attack him, every member of the police, the Army, Navy and Air Force, will be looking for us."

"*Ardhe,* Spiro." It was Cerrik calling softly, and pointing. Jakova ran out of the ruins to get a better view of the road leading up to the villa. Leeming was behind him.

A black twenty-seater bus, full of uniformed armed policemen appeared up the road and halted outside the villa's main gate. About a dozen men got out, marched into the grounds and immediately made a careful tour of the area, searching the bushes and low hedges behind the walls. They all ended up at the rear gate. The guard in this sentry box now joined the group and another man took up his vacated position. They then moved off in single file around the east side of the house and out the front gate. The guard in front exchanged places with another of the new arrivals, and then the remainder moved back to the bus, which drove off.

Leeming looked at his watch. "We'll have to check whether this changing of the guard is at the same time each lunch hour."

Jakova waited a moment, then said, "What d'you think?"

Leeming shrugged. "I didn't calculate he'd put so much effort into his own security—that house looks like it's designed to prevent him from being kidnapped. But that's what we have to do." He nodded toward the villa. "And that's where we have to do it."

22

MACKERRAS RENDEZVOUSED WITH THE bald-headed man whom Leeming had met in the swimming pool at the Club Militaire, for their monthly meeting at the Gallerie Claude Bernard in rue des Beaux Arts. The general followed the tall sixty-year-old man around the empty gallery. He had not known that the man liked modern art.

"I buy a couple of paintings a year, freight them to some damn storage company in Chicago. It's getting harder to find just one good picture a year."

The bald man seemed nervous this evening, walked more stiffly than usual with his cane. A decade back the man had spent two years in Lubianka Prison in Moscow. They had broken his body, but his mind had survived. He had been undergoing therapy for the last ten years, but he had not been able to repair the ravages of his prison treatment. Mackerras could tell by the way the man used his stick, lightly, or leaning on it heavily, whether or not he was in pain.

"Leeming's in Albania," Mackerras said. "I give him a half chance."

"Do you?" the man responded, in a vague way. He was standing in front of a large impressionist oil portrait of some medieval bishop. " 'Bacon, Francis.' " The man read from the typed sheet he was carrying. His voice was harsh, as if he had spent a lot of his life shouting at people. "What do you think of the painting, Mackerras? I always feel art should be more 'obscura' and less 'camera.' I'm no goddam intellectual but I say good art is the selection of the elements to hide. You understand?"

Mackerras did not. "What happens if Leeming does line up the hit?"

"What happens?" The bald man returned the general's question, perhaps wanting amplification of it.

"If Leeming does succeed I have to know how we handle Buckman."

" 'Bacon, Francis. Portuguese Navigator.' Look at this picture." The large man snorted. "The man looks like he has a T-bone steak for a face. You ever read the writings of the Portuguese navigators—Da Gama, Bartholomew Dias?"

Mackerras looked at the bold black and pink colors of the portrait.

"That's no Portuguese navigator." The bald man paused for a moment, thinking, then he said, "They were half men, half gods. They made seamanship a religion. You should read Da Gama. He says things I feel about life. It's not the journey out to discover new lands that's the point of it. It's the journey home, when a man may learn his own meridians and chart the contours of his soul."

"You are avoiding giving me a lead on this," Mackerras said coldly. "And I need it. What happens to Buckman if Leeming succeeds in a hit?"

"General, I'll give you my opinion." The bald man was still glowering at the seaman's portrait. "Suppose it's bingo and your Colonel Leeming holds the winning card, then you will have a very short while to either reeducate Buckman, or plan his future maybe in the manner that Mister Van Dhoc deals with his problems. But really, for Leeming to succeed he has to have more than one winning card. My honest opinion is that he won't survive in Albania more than a few days."

23

IT WAS THREE P.M. Jakova, with Leeming and Skendi sitting alongside him on the bench seat, drove the truck rattling toward the coast. Skendi had an old uncle, a retired lighthouse keeper, who lived in a disused lighthouse on the Kep Palit promontory north of Port Durres. The man still had a job as the watchman over a nearby installation of rusting iron sheds containing Coast Guard equipment, buoys and weather beacons. Jakova had decided that if they succeeded in kidnapping Kellezi he could be hidden and interrogated here.

They drove through heavy rain west to the coast. The sprawl of rusting nissen huts was two hundred yards from the foreshore and the blistered white column of the disused lighthouse. Skendi and Jakova went off to talk to the uncle, leaving Leeming in the truck. They returned twenty minutes later with two keys, one for the gate in the wire fence, the other for the hut which was about forty feet long and fifteen feet wide. The place smelled of damp and the shelves of cork lifebelts stacked along the walls. There were a half-dozen battered glass skylights set into the hut, but no windows through which they could be observed.

"It's a good place, eh?" Jakova said.

Leeming nodded. "What did you tell the uncle?"

"We want to store black-market goods. We gave him some money." Jakova changed tack. "We'd like to know, when do we hear your plans for the kidnap?"

"Tomorrow morning you'll have my decisions." He looked at his watch. "I must make radio contact with Mackerras."

Jakova had hidden the wireless transmitter in a compartment in the rear floor of the van. Leeming didn't say anything while he set up the radio, and Jakova—deciding that he wanted privacy—took Skendi by the hand and strolled back across the sand.

In the back of the truck Leeming inserted a tape cassette into the radio deck and pushed a transmit button. The cassette would send out his call sign and tune the wave band automatically. A moment later the cassette snapped out. He picked up the thin plastic microphone and spoke into it. "Marauder One. Reception?"

"Marauder Two." It was Mackerras' voice. "Reception one hundred over."

"Marauder One. On locale, on schedule. I've just come from nearly colliding with Target A"

"Explain."

"I was following Target B. Target A was in a car behind Target B. I lost him."

"Pity." Mackerras made the word sound flat and critical.

"So I'm in square one searching for A. Target B is heavily secured. Our troop here concern me. They're like a bunch of Berber bandits. Some questionable enthusiasm. Poor equipment. Amateurish. But I'll do my piece. Over."

Mackerras' voice came back sharp. "You must understand, it's meant to be amateursville. That's the whole point. In the event some members are caught it must look like a group of lunatics. If it went wrong and was identified as a highly professional operation routed through our side, it could start World War Three."

Leeming was silent a moment. Then he said, "Copy."

"Anything else?"

"Negative. Will stay in contact."

"Do that. Over and out."

24

SKENDI'S APARTMENT WAS IN a tall prewar building squeezed between two modern office blocks. The entrance hall was dark, paneled in wood now chipped and scarred. Jakova pointed upward. "No elevator. Five floors up."

Leeming began the climb. The high ceilings of the apartments made for a lot of steps and by the time he'd reached the fifth floor he was out of breath. Skendi gestured them in wordlessly. The living was crammed with furniture and crude shelving filled with books. A gas fire burned low in front of an old iron mantelpiece. She made dinner for Leeming, Haziz and Jakova. Cerrik was still out watching the villa. The cousins Pilo and Dmitri had gone off to their homes. They had just finished the meal, and Jakova had opened still another bottle of wine, when Leeming decided to raise the question of Kellezi's interrogation.

"We've been talking about that," Jakova said gently. "After we have questioned him, we will probably just kill him."

Leeming was astounded. The man was serious. "What the hell d'you mean? We worked out the plan in detail. I get the information you want, we push two tablets of Senibral down his throat, deliver him back near his villa. He's found blundering around the streets in the middle of the night. For a week nothing he says makes sense, so no one's out hunting us. The drug's undetectable. They'll conclude he's had a mental breakdown. That was always the plan."

Jakova said it softly, so quietly that at first Leeming thought he'd misunderstood, "Maybe we're not doing this for your General Mackerras and his little pots of gold. Maybe we were always in this to take your excellent M40's, your U-V night sights, grab him, make him talk, then kill him. Perhaps we are part of a completely different vendetta from yours, Leeming."

Leeming started his arguments, measuring his points, pressing them home, making sure that Jakova was following. But the man made no commitment and finally at one o'clock in the morning announced he was leaving. He got unsteadily to his feet.

"This is my final word," Leeming said. "If I seriously thought there was a chance that you were going to kill this man, I'm through."

"We talk more of this in the morning," Jakova said.

"I want your answer now," Leeming said sharply. "He's not to be killed."

"Yes, probably." Jakova smiled drunkenly. "We'll talk tomorrow. I'll be here seven A.M."

Jakova and Haziz left. Skendi went off into the kitchen. There was the sound of running water, the kettle boiling, and dishes clattering.

Leeming poured himself another glass of wine allowing his anger free reign. Anger at Jakova, and more— anger at himself for not realizing that of course they wouldn't be satisfied just with information. He should have understood. He had not succeeded in logical argument, so he'd have to find another approach.

Skendi had finished in the kitchen, switched out the kitchen light and gone to her bedroom. There was no light coming from the bedroom and the hall was in darkness. He was sitting on the long sofa next to the fire. Jakova had said this would be Leeming's bed and Skendi had put out a couple of folded blankets. He got up and spread them over the sofa. He was aware of the unsteadiness of his feet, the clumsiness of his movements as he pulled off his shirt and trousers, sat down in his underpants, raised his glass and clinked it to the bottle. It was probably that sound which she heard in her bedroom.

He was sitting there in his underpants when he heard a slight noise behind him. She was standing there. She had a faded old terrycloth bathrobe thrown round her shoulders. She stood still, just looking at him, no speculation in her eyes, no calculation. And yet her signal was obvious.

He put the half-full glass of wine on the floor and stood up. He knew he was drunk and he vaguely recalled Jakova's warning to stay away from her. He knew there would be an important role for the girl in the days to come which he might compromise now. But even more he knew he needed her. He had a sudden memory of her that morning in Cerrik's house, seeing her there, the naked top of her body with the squared strength of her shoulders, the firm rise of her breasts. He knew he was drunk, but even sober he would not have the resolve to turn her away.

She was still standing in the doorway. He put out his hand. Her hand extended, releasing the front of her robe. She was naked underneath. Without words she led him to her room.

She closed the wooden shutters, let the robe slip from her shoulders and climbed into the bed. He took off his pants and moved beside her, feeling no compulsion to rush things. The decision had been made that they would make love and there was a whole night before them.

He listened to the vague sounds of the night outside, a moment's collision of car horns a few streets away, the rattle of an empty train heading for a terminal. He was aware of her breathing. It was getting deeper, and there was a slight movement in her body. He reached out and

found her arm and traced his fingers down to her hand
which was probing between her legs. He waited a minute until he heard a soft moan, and then took her hand
firmly and pulled it aside, moving his body across hers.

She made such a sharp intake of breath that he wondered if he'd hurt her. And then she was still, as he
started to make love to her. He pulled himself up from
her body, studied her face. Her eyes were pressed
tightly closed. She opened them. She was trying to signal something with the mixture of pain and need in her
expression, but he didn't know what it was.

Suddenly she slid from under him and pushed him
back. He saw what she wanted, and he lay on his back
as she moved on top of him. She pushed herself down
so hard that he felt that for him this would be an experience on the borderline of pain. She started to work her
body against his, making shocked gasps as she felt the
passions of her own needs. But there was something else
there that he had never encountered before and he realized why she had chosen this position. It was to punish herself for the feelings that had betrayed her own
loyalties.

She reached her climax and a second later he joined
her. They lay almost unmoving for half an hour. Then
she pulled her body up and looked at him, little happi-
ness on her face. Her head came up and she laid it on
his chest. Then slowly she started to move it down. This
time he took her firmly around the waist and put her on
her back. He took his time and she too seemed to have
calmed, but when he raised his head and looked at her
she didn't react fast enough to disguise her tears. There
was one photograph in the room on the bedside table.
She had been making love to him while studying the
face of her dead husband.

He tried to tell her it was all right, that he understood
what she must be going through. But he knew the situation was not salvageable. Even if he spoke her language
he would not be able to comfort her. She had moved

away from him, pulled up the blanket to cover her na-
kedness, and closed her eyes. He watched her face for a
few minutes more, as the tears poured out through her
closed eyelids.

25

OUTSIDE THE SMALL WINDOW of the sitting room, dark-gray clouds were slowly moving across Tiranha. It had started to drizzle. Leeming finished his coffee and put it down. "I've worked out how we do it," he said.

Although only Jakova knew English, something in Leeming's voice made them all look at him. "It's a plan that involves a lot of risk, but I believe that is inevitable. We've studied Kellezi's villa, his office building, the movements around them. I see only one moment in his routine when he's vulnerable."

"When?" Jakova asked.

Leeming didn't answer. "Let me tell you a story," he said. "I had a friend who was an Intelligence officer in 'Nam. Early in the war he was given the job of investigating a report that the captain of Division Nine, Saigon Police, was collaborating with the Viet Cong—and that most of the man's junior officers were also collaborators. The U.S. Army viewed this with very serious concern."

"What has this to do with Kellezi?"

"Wait." Leeming gently quieted Jakova's impatience. "The police captain looked like a thoroughgoing capitalist—he'd imported a big Toyota station wagon from Hong Kong, he had a house on the coast at Vung Tau, and a little fiberglass yacht at the bottom of its garden. The problem was he could not be arrested on circumstantial evidence. So it was decided to secretly abduct him for questioning by Army Intelligence. The second

problem was that obviously as soon as the man was reported missing the entire Saigon Police Force, an effi-
cient group of guys, would be making this their number-
one case."

Jakova started eating again but he was listening.

"My friend studied the man for some time and came
up with an idea. The police captain used to meet four of
his collaborators aboard his little yacht once a week.
They'd all climb into the boat which sat on its trestle at
the bottom of the guy's back lot. My friend decided to
wait till they were on board, and blow up the yacht.
First with a percussion charge that would stun everybody inside. Then with an explosive to make one of the
biggest bangs in the war."

"I'm not following you," Jakova said, his mouth full.

"The police captain was abducted semiconscious between the first explosion and the second. The second
explosion didn't leave a piece of skin, or bone or fiberglass bigger than a postage stamp."

"How does this apply to Kellezi?"

"There's a moment when Kellezi's potentially vulnerable. If we can make it look as if he's been killed, we
can hold him a few hours, get all the information we
want, and then release him doped on Senibral. When he
reappears after the authorities have concluded he's
dead, I reckon that'll blunt the intensity of the hunt for
us." Jakova nodded at last and began to translate for
the others.

Although Cerrik knew a bit about explosives, Leeming decided to make the bombs himself. They sat
around and watched him, chatting quietly among themselves. He was struck by how curiously domestic the
scene seemed, with Skendi brewing coffee, and the
good-looking one—Haziz—going out for fresh bread
and newspapers after he'd brought up the gelignite from
the truck.

The explosive was Dow Concentrate. Buckman had
mentioned the flash coefficient was exactly twice the
normal rate for mining-grade explosive. Leeming
needed two types of containers. The first bomb could

be housed in an empty olive oil tin Skendi found in her kitchen. He wanted the stunning effect of the blast rather than the lethal effect of a contained bomb. For the second Jakova suggested placing five pounds of gelignite in an old World War Two steel jerrycan that he had in the back of the truck.

The bombs were assembled and ready sitting on the washboard in the kitchen by lunchtime. As soon as they had been completed, Leeming noted a slight rise in the tension in the room, not because of the proximity of powerful explosive devices but probably, he felt, because the making of the devices committed them all to the confrontation.

26

PILO'S ORDERS WERE TO park the first car a hundred yards down the road from the tobacco-drying plant at exactly five-oh-five. He raised the hood and started tinkering with a screwdriver inside the engine compartment. To anyone passing by it was to appear that the Skoda had broken down. As it happened none of the fifty or so workers from the tobacco plant were to be seen, and there was little traffic on the main road.

Leeming, Skendi and Jakova drove past the factory at five-ten in the second car and turned into the narrow lane which led up to the villa. Skendi and Leeming climbed out quickly. Dmitri, Huziz and Cerrik were already there with the two bombs, sheltering behind some low bushes.

Leeming, carrying the monocular, ran past them, his feet scattering the rotting wet leaves of last fall, up to a vantage point he had selected yesterday from the church ruins. This aerie, on a small rock outcrop of the hill, gave him some view of the exterior walls of the villa three hundred yards away, and would allow him to see Kellezi's car, when it approached.

There was a large cypress tree marking the rock outcrop. He moved through some bushes at its base, put up the monocular and started a three-hundred and sixty degree pan from the walls of the villa down through the trees to check Jakova's preparations. He had maneuvered the car around, and then backed it into a little glade of trees just off the lane.

As Leeming continued to pan the monocular, he could see that Cerrik had the first explosive device ready and waiting in his hands. He checked his watch. They were all in position and it was five-thirteen. Now to sit it out. Kellezi would return from his office between five-forty-five and six, if he followed last night's timing. If he was delayed beyond six-thirty then they would call it all off for today. For their escape they needed some fast driving in thin traffic. Jakova had said that by six-thirty the road to the coast would be busy with rush-hour traffic.

Looking down on the landscape, the group checked into their positions below, Leeming had a sudden jolt of memory as he thought of himself at another ambush. It would always be a vivid recollection, because he remembered the VC patrol was so close he could actually see the expressions on individual faces as they died. They were walking back into their hideout in some forest caves where they had lived for years. Leeming had been given the intelligence report, personally taken from some men in the forest, attacked and killed the four VC standing guard over the caves, then ordered his men inside to await the return of the VC. They'd arrived at dusk. He could remember their voices, high-spirited, hungry for their suppers. Their last meal had been the hail of fire.

He looked back at the Kellezi villa, studied the sentry box on the front gate. He could just make out the dark shape of the man seated inside. He made one final calculation—how long it would take for that guard to decide to leave his post and run down the lane to the scene of the ambush. Would he make the decision quickly, in which case he would be on the scene in thirty seconds, or would he pause to make the phone call reporting the explosions? Leeming reckoned he would do the latter.

He started down again, jogging through the trees and mud. As he neared Cerrik, Jakova was gesturing Haziz to move the car forward into the lane.

Leeming handed the monocular to Dmitri who lumbered off, feet crashing through the undergrowth, directly down to the point where the lane met the main road. He was to signal when Kellezi's car approached.

Leeming took the first bomb out of Cerrik's hands and put it down on the carpet of leaves. He pulled out a box of matches, removed one and then cautiously laid the box and the match down on the flat top of the olive oil tin.

Jakova had meanwhile guided Haziz's parking of the Skoda. The car was now halted sideways blocking the lane. Kellezi's driver would come off the main road, get halfway into the corner and then see his way blocked. The calculation was that he would slam on the brakes, the Lada would stop, and the bomb in the olive oil tin could be thrown at the car.

Haziz remained behind the steering wheel, the engine ticking over. He was to be ready at a second's notice to reverse into the original position behind the trees if Dmitri spotted any other vehicle coming off the main road and heading up toward the villa. Dmitri had a gymnast's whistle. The signal was to be one blow for Kellezi's car approaching, two blows for any other traffic leaving the main road.

Jakova opened the trunk and pulled out the jerrycan bomb. Carefully cradling it in his arms, he started to bring it across to Leeming when he froze in mid-stride. Dmitri had blown once on the whistle, no mistaking that. Kellezi's car was arriving half an hour earlier than they'd calculated.

Leeming moved fast and with precision. He lifted the olive oil tin up and ran out into the middle of the lane. With one eye on the parked Skoda ten yards away, he placed the bomb in the middle of the road, went down on his knees striking the match on the box. Out of the corner of his eye he could see the others scatter for cover, Haziz half falling out of the car and hurtling past him.

He saw a blur that was Skendi, before she vanished into the trees north of the lane. He lighted the akracord fuse. His hands were not trembling. It was as if he was putting a match to some paraffin stove at a country cookout. He saw the phosphorus catch and sparkle, was on his feet immediately running as if the fuse had a second's duration, not five, up the slope toward the first grouping of trees where he could see Jakova and Cerrik, their faces already flat in the mud waiting for the bang. He sprinted on a dozen feet past them, grabbed up an M40 from where Cerrik had propped it against a tree and threw himself flat.

The Lada station wagon turned the corner of the lane, went into a fast skid, ran over the bomb and blew up. The car spiraled up and over and crashed down on its roof.

There was a moment of silence. The somersault had broken open the rear tailgate of the station wagon. Suddenly out of the back of the vehicle, barking hysterically, came a huge dog. For a second Leeming was caught off balance. It was the dog he'd seen guarding the house. For some reason Kellezi had taken it into town, or maybe the chauffeur had taken it along on the ride to collect Kellezi.

The animal, wild-eyed and panicked by the explosion, took off, running flat-out up the hill. Haziz was first to the car, Cerrik second. They ran headlong at it and then threw themselves flat down on the ground to each side of it. There were four stunned men inside, the chauffeur, Kellezi and two bodyguards. Only the chauffeur was unconscious—the two bodyguards and Kellezi were staring into the barrels of the M40's.

Leeming pulled open the half-buckled front door, grabbed at Kellezi's legs and dragged him roughly out. He hoisted him to his feet. Jakova was covering the man with his gun. Haziz had meanwhile run back and climbed into the parked Skoda.

Leeming ticked off the seconds as the Skoda tore mud and grit from the lane's surface, screeched about in a half circle and came racing back to the capsized Lada. Leeming picked up the M40 and pressing the barrel into Kellezi's neck, gestured him to get quickly into the back of the car.

The chauffeur regained consciousness and started to scream loudly in pain. Jakova had by now carefully positioned the jerrycan bomb on top of the upturned car. He had matches in his hand. He turned and looked to Leeming for his order. Suddenly the huge dog was back and running wildly among them. Dmitri reacted, swung his M40 and was about to fire when Leeming grabbed aside the barrel of the gun.

"No!" he shouted. He spun round on Jakova. "Translate. We can't have the shot body of a dog lying near to the blown-up car. They'll think if the dog got away, maybe Kellezi got away."

Jakova started to shout a translation at Dmitri. Meanwhile the dog was up on its hind legs pawing the rear door of the Skoda, trying to get at its master.

"Put it in," Leeming yelled. He'd grabbed the matches away from Jakova. "Put the dog in the car. We'll kill it later."

They could all hear the urgent horn blasts from Pilo, who'd brought the second Skoda up from outside the tobacco-processing plant and had repositioned it, engine revving, fifty yards down the lane.

"Get the dog in."

Jakova and Dmitri opened the door of the car. The huge dog pushed itself in on Kellezi, starting to paw and lick at the man's face.

Leeming lighted a match, lighted the fuse. "Go!" he shouted to Dmitri, Cerrik and Skendi.

The two men and the girl set off sprinting down the lane. Leeming got into the car. Jakova was second, throwing himself into the driver's seat. The car accelerated, spinning on a stream of mud. Leeming angled himself around, so that with his right hand he could hold the M40 low, pointed it at Kellezi's stomach. He got one last look at the upturned Lada. The two guards inside were trying to disentangle themselves, too late to get out, the last spate of agonized screams came from the injured chauffeur.

Jakova hurtled the car lurching down the lane and spun it around the corner onto the main road, and then was accelerating again to catch up with Pilo. From a distance of a hundred and fifty yards the explosion rocked Jakova's car. Leeming calculated the detonation would have stripped the Lada into thousands of pieces of metal, and shredded the human bodies inside into a thousand tiny pieces of unrecognizable flesh and bone.

The road to Kep Palit was fairly busy with traffic. Leeming hardly saw it, his eyes glued to the man in the back. He knew Kellezi was thinking that whoever these mad men were they would obviously end up killing him. And if this was the case, he should make his play at the first chance. One lurch of the car, a pothole in the road, the big dog altering its position, and then the move. The animal was getting restless and starting to shift its great bulk around. And it had begun to bark again, unhappy because its master wasn't playing with it.

"There's going to be an accident with the dog," Jakova said through gritted teeth. "We kill it. I'll find a turnoff."

"Keep driving," Leeming ordered. "Keep going."

The Skoda with Pilo, Skendi, Haziz and Dmitri in it had allowed Jakova to overtake it and was now forming a rear guard. The drive was just beginning to seem endless when the traffic thinned out and Leeming could smell the sea. Jakova turned the car off the main Durres road and found the path that curved through the grass dunes along the coast. Ten minutes later they were there, parking in the wilderness by the huts. Skendi went off to check if her uncle was at home and, if he was, to keep him occupied until the cars were parked out of sight.

Meanwhile Leeming, Jakova, Kellezi and the dog had gotten out of the Skoda, and the dog was bounding and barking around, exploring the sands. Jakova opened the padlock on the gate in the wire fencing, and Haziz drove both the cars in behind the huts. Jakova then opened up the one with the lifebelts in it.

"Take Kellezi. I'll kill the dog." He handed Leeming the Smith and Wesson he'd carried. Leeming gave him the M40.

"Try and do it with a single shot, or no more than two. I'm worried you'll be heard," Leeming warned.

The dog had now disappeared around the back of some huts. Jakova set off after it.

Leeming prodded Kellezi in the back and they stepped into the hut. They heard the sound of a shot. A yelp. Another shot, and then silence.

Leeming motioned the man to be seated on a pile of lifebelts. Kellezi had shown no reaction to the sound of his dog being killed. Jakova walked into the shed.

"Is the dog dead?"

"It's kicking, but it's dying. You said no more than two shots."

"If you're sure it's dying, leave it."

His order was to prove a fatal mistake. The dog was not to die for several hours.

27

FOR HALF AN HOUR Leeming sat on a sandbank outside the nissen hut with the tool kit from the Skoda, making adjustments to the bullets. He found the knack of twisting the end of the screwdriver between the lead and the casings and slowly, gently, working the two apart. Then he emptied the contents onto the sand. The rest of them were inside the hut. Jakova had decided to start the proceedings by softening up Kellezi, slapping him around, firing off the questions about the catalog of missing people.

The noise of the beating carried to Leeming where he worked. When he finished, he got up, brushed the sand off his hands, walked into the hut. Kellezi was tied by a rope to one of the iron girder side-supports. His face was now lopsided with bruising. Blood from the punches had run down from his lips and chin to stain his collar, but his expression was still resolute, defiant.

"He's told us nothing," Jakova said.

"Two of you hold his head. One of you get his mouth open," Leeming said softly.

Jakova translated. Dmitri and Haziz gripped the man's head. Jakova pulled up the man's nose and pushed down his chin. Kellezi's mouth opened. Leeming took the Smith and Wesson .380 and broke it open. He saw Kellezi's eyes on the gun as he revealed that the revolver was empty. Then he carefully loaded a bullet into the gun. He snapped the gun together again.

He put the gun barrel into the man's mouth. "Ask him where Van Dhoc is?"

Jakova asked the question. No sound but rasped breathing from Kellezi.

Leeming spun the chambers of the gun and pulled the trigger. A loud click.

Kellezi's forehead broke out in a sweat.

"Ask him again."

Jakova repeated the question.

Still no indication of an answer, but a strangled sound from Kellezi.

Leeming spun the chambers, paused, then pulled the trigger. A click.

Now Cerrik and Pilo were talking fast to Jakova. Leeming could guess what they were saying. They didn't want Kellezi dead until he'd divulged a whole lot of information. Their genuine worry at Leeming's game of Russian roulette communicated itself to Kellezi.

"Ask him again."

Jakova barked the same question at Kellezi but his eyes were on Leeming, uncertain.

Kellezi said nothing.

Leeming spun the chambers of the Smith and Wesson, saw Kellezi's teeth close and grind on the barrel, waiting for death, sweat pouring from his forehead. Then suddenly his courage was gone and he was babbling, his teeth clicking on the steel of the barrel. Leeming took the pistol out of the man's mouth.

"Van Dhoc," Jakova translated Kellezi's words, "is in the citadel at Scutari. He promises you that is the truth. He says, go to the Scutari citadel. You will find Van Dhoc there."

"D'you believe him?" Leeming asked. "Is there a citadel at Scutari?"

"Yes, a famous one," Jakova said.

"Can he be more precise than that? Whereabouts in the citadel?"

Jakova translated. The man babbled on again.

"He says that is all he knows. There is accommodation in the citadel. The Vietnamese is there. I think he's telling the truth," Jakova said. "And I think that's a dangerous game you were playing. The first bullet could have killed him and all our efforts would have been wasted."

Leeming gestured to Jakova to follow and turned and walked out of the hut. They stopped on the sand. "The bullet was a dud. I opened it, took out the explosive." He handed Jakova the doctored bullet.

Jakova looked at it, unbelieving. Then he started to laugh. "I must tell the others."

"Don't let Kellezi know till he's answered your questions."

"Of course."

Jakova went to the door and called them by name, except Pilo, who was left standing guard. When Jakova finished translating the three men burst out laughing, the tension of the hours leading up to the kidnap now evaporating, in loud rolling bellows. Skendi didn't seem so amused. The laughter ended and for a second there was silence. Then they heard from inside the hut the sound of Kellezi's weeping.

"I'll tell you how to get him to talk." Leeming had sat down on a rusting oil drum. "All of you—take it in ten-minute relays. Shout anything at him for a half-hour, but particularly questions you know he can't answer—to disorient him. Then I'll come in and ask the specific questions you want answered. Maybe start the ball rolling with Skendi." Leeming had seen her go back into the hut.

Suddenly Pilo walked out of the hut. Leeming was frozen to the spot as he heard the bark of an M40, three distinct shots, and he and all of them realized Skendi had somehow gotten Pilo to give her his gun, maybe telling him he was needed outside, and now she was in the hut killing the minister.

It was like frames from a movie breaking down on the screen, the movements animated, but jerky. And the picture displayed was so horrifying that none of them standing outside could believe it. Kellezi appeared and paused for a second in the doorway. Skendi's first shot had blown open a huge bloodied cloth flap below the breast pocket of his jacket. The second had sliced through his left wrist, completely severing his hand except for a small strip of flesh still joining the dangling hand to the wrist. Kellezi raised the stump with the hand dangling off it in some gesture of supplication, as if he knew he shouldn't be dying—that it would not be their plan to kill him yet. It must be the girl whose hatred, trembling through her body, so possessed her she couldn't even hold a gun straight.

Mortally injured, Kellezi stumbled out onto the sand, somehow kept to his feet, veered left, and with the last reserves in his body ran ten steps forward, and then his back blew open and shredded in blood as Skendi, now in control of the gun's aim, fired the third burst from the door of the hut.

The rest of them, coming out of shock, began moving toward her, but their reactions were circumscribed, hesitant because already they knew it was too late.

Skendi dropped the M40, turned and walked back into the hut. Leeming and the others changed direction as if someone had given an order. They moved uncertainly across the sand to the smashed body.

Leeming understood. Skendi had been present the night they had talked about drugging Kellezi, releasing him—letting her husband's murderer survive. She had known this was their plan and had acted at the first opportunity.

He looked down. It was not the sight of the bullet mutilations that sickened him, it was the realization that somehow the odds against the mission's success had been increased a thousandfold now, and the knowledge, something more than intuition, that this man's death would doom them all.

28

BUCKMAN SPOTTED THEM IN the rue de Rivoli. He'd been standing outside the shopping arcade across from the Palais du Louvre trying to find a cab in the lunchtime traffic, when he realized that he'd seen both men a quarter of an hour earlier. He had been walking out of a coffee shop off Place Caire and had nearly collided with the taller of the two who was wearing a gray leather hat and gray gabardine raincoat. His companion had a black wool overcoat and one of the large white umbrellas that were popular at French racetracks. Buckman knew that the men who fifteen minutes before had been in a back street square were unlikely to be standing behind a group of columns in the arcade, unless they had been following him.

While he debated what to do a cab pulled up for him. He gave his own address in Faubourg St. Honoré and then managed a quick sidelong look at the two. One of the men had already walked out from behind a column to hail another taxi.

The cab wound its way in darts and horn bursts up Faubourg St. Honoré to the top. Buckman climbed out at the Matignon junction and in his nervousness overtipped the cabby. He was rewarded with a smiling mouthful of broken teeth. He went in his front door, skipped the elevator, and climbed the two floors to his apartment. He hoped that he'd be able to find his camera and that there would be some film in it.

It was in a drawer of the hi-fi bureau where he kept

his cassette tapes. He remembered he had used it recently, taken a couple of flashbulb photographs of the boy Tod one night when they were both drunk. But the photographs were innocent enough. They were of Tod sitting in a dressing gown on the edge of the bed.

The camera was a palm-size German Minox. Zeiss lens, twenty exposures on 35mm film. He checked. There was plenty of film left. He went to the window, looked through the nylon curtains down to the street. They were there, chatting busily to each other, looking in the broad window of a men's store. It was a warm day. They would be hot in their heavy coats.

He took the Minox out of its leather pouch, wound the film forward, then dropped the camera in his pocket. He walked out of his apartment and carefully snapped the two Yale deadlocks which he rarely used. If these people were that interested in his business, his apartment was a possible target. He was intrigued to see what they might make out of two locks in the solid oak door.

He wanted an open space to use the camera. He headed toward the Parc Monceau, thinking he'd need at least one snapshot within twenty feet of his subjects, not that easy to manage because he was sure the instant they saw what he was doing they'd turn and run. And he had to have a clear shot of the two faces in order to formally request General Mackerras to investigate the incident through Washington, and come up with the name of the CIA operative who had assigned the tail. Then as an official of G2 he would go calling on the CIA with an Army lawyer. He figured he'd enjoy that part of it.

He walked into Monceau, turned right and moved at a leisurely pace toward a temporary bandstand near the Pavillon de Chartres. Within half an hour there would be the first of the office workers seeking out their benches, with their tin boxes of sandwiches and plastic half-liters of *vin ordinaire,* but for the moment the park was deserted. The path he was on had been relaid within the last week or so, giving a different sound to his shoes scattering stones.

He heard them behind him—maybe thirty, forty feet back as he walked out of the avenue of trees into the open. His hand reached into his pocket and maneuvered the Minox around until he was satisfied he'd gotten the proper grip on it. Then in one movement he turned, grabbed the camera up to his eye, and pressed the shutter.

He stood there stock-still. There was no one behind him. His eyes searched the park. He saw a couple of pigeons lift themselves, only half bothered, out of the path of an approaching dog. He saw a nurse coming in the gates with two young children sitting tandem in a pram. He wondered if he'd gone mad, but he knew he hadn't. He knew he'd heard those two sets of footfalls. He stood there for a minute, impotent. Then for no apparent reason a wave of fear overtook him making his legs and hands tremble, and he felt the sudden wetness of cold sweat on his face.

29

RAIN HAULED A GRAY veil over the skies that kept darkening as they headed north. The drive from Tiranha to Scutari took four hours in the overheating truck. Leeming sat in front with the silent Jakova, his mind churning over the problems born out of the pointless killing. By the time they reached the outskirts of Scutari he'd decided that months from now, when the time came to weigh and compare the separate problems of the Albanian venture, Kellezi's murder would probably rate little alongside the crises to come. And the fact was he'd gotten what he wanted—the whereabouts of Dhoc. Why should the huge search which no doubt would be initiated in Tiranha after the man's disappearance affect the efforts of the group in Scutari? It had happened. Kellezi was dead. Leeming himself had buried him in a trench between sand dunes on the Kep Palit beach.

He thought about the changes in the girl from the moment she'd shot Kellezi. First fear—and Leeming had realized that she was frightened her death would follow, that one of the group would slay her. Then, when the group returned from the beach to her apartment to conduct a post-mortem, she had gone into shock. She went to her bedroom, weeping hysterically. She kept saying, again and again, "He killed my husband, he killed Petrit." An hour later she came out of the bedroom. The tears were over and there was a firm line to her mouth. Leeming guessed she'd worked it out, concluded that what she had done was right. Her new strength intimidated the others. Leeming stepped into the row and told Jakova to translate his orders to them. He made it short and to the point. The crisis was over. Kellezi was dead, but they had killed him and had gotten away with it. He was sure if they stayed in Albania the police would sooner or later catch them. If they were interested, he offered escape to Europe or the U.S. via the Feiseler—but only after Van Dhoc had been located and dealt with. At midnight, when the men left, Jakova told Leeming he must return with him and sleep the night in Cerrik's place. It was as if he thought Leeming left alone in the apartment might execute the girl. They all agreed to meet at eight A.M. and take the truck to the citadel.

The rain changed to hail at Leeming's first sight of Scutari. On the topmost rise, silhouetted against the soaking gray clouds, he could see the black mass of the half-mile-long building dominating the town below. On the ride, Jakova had told him about the town which he'd visited a half-dozen times in his life. It was one of the oldest in Albania. The Romans had originally destroyed and rebuilt it. They were kicked out in the fifth century by the Byzantines, who centuries later sold the city to the Venetians, hoping they could protect it from the Turks. They failed. In the fifteenth century the Venetian-Turkish treaty handed over Scutari, lock, stock and barrel, to the Eastern invaders. The inhabitants repaired to the citadel and a siege started which went on for four years. The Turks eventually allowed those in the citadel to walk out, armed and unharmed, though they were later to level everything within. In the eighteenth century Scutari came back on the map as a major trading center between East and West, and this was the period when much new building was added, in the Turkish style. Low houses, iron-barred windows, steel-studded doors. And pricking the skyline the minarets of the Muslims and the pinnacles and crosses of the Christians.

Leeming thought about how one of them would die there, Dhoc or himself. Or maybe both or all of them. He, who had never gone as a pessimist into battle, doubted now. Because, when he came to think of it, not one single thing that had happened since he'd arrived in Albania had gone right.

Around the same time as Leeming and the others were leaving for Scutari, Skendi's uncle, the retired lighthouse keeper, heard a dog howling. He walked from the lighthouse down to the storage huts, went into the compound and saw the dog. It had survived the night and dragged itself from the dune where it had collapsed across twenty yards of sand to the Kellezi burial mound. With the last energy of its life it dug two feet down through the sand to expose part of the face and body.

Old Kocho saw the dying dog and the dead body, and immediately marched off across the dunes half a mile to a phone booth on the coast road. He called the police. He hadn't recognized the face of the man, but even before the two policemen arrived in a Lada, he was frightened. He knew the last persons inside the nissen area were his grandniece, Skendi, and her friend. Two days back they'd asked for a hut to store black-market goods. The old man decided that whatever happened, he would not relate that to the authorities.

The two policemen arrived casually, but as soon as they recognized the face of the victim they became nervous, arrested Kocho, and while one of them shouted questions, the other went off for reinforcements. Within an hour there were over a hundred men combing the dunes, the huts, photographing everything including some bullet casings, and finally surveying the area with a light spotter plane.

Two hours after this the first politicians arrived—a half a dozen of them. They questioned the policemen, Kocho, and then each other. Then they went into a huddle with the head of the Criminal Investigation Bureau of the Department of Internal Security. The spent shells from Jakova's gun had been taken off by helicopter to the Bureau's forensic laboratory in the capital. Within two hours the police and the politicians at the site were in possession of some worrying news which Skendi's uncle was able to pass on to Jakova the next day. The shell casings found were of a highly unusual .400 caliber. The Tiranha laboratory put in a telephone call to an arms supplier in Switzerland and learned that the .400 caliber was the very latest development out of the American Remington arms factory—so recent that the arms were not in general distribution but might possibly be available to a specialist unit in the U.S. Forces.

Periodically when the police or politicians had a spare moment they came back to threaten and question Kocho. His visible fear in any other country would have automatically indicated guilt, but fear when confronted by the police was considered a natural reaction in Albania. They would release him later in the day.

At two o'clock they learned of the American manufacture of the gun. The politicians and police stood around debating what was currently going on in Albania that would interest the Americans. Kocho heard the name Van Dhoc. At four P.M. a helicopter landed on the beach next to his lighthouse and a tall man with Chinese features stepped out. He was accompanied by two *shteti* guards and a translator.

Kocho listened. The chief of the Criminal Investigation Bureau questioned the Vietnamese quietly and with respect. Van Dhoc did not believe that his recent operation in the United States might have caused the Americans to murder Kellezi, though it might be possible as there was nothing in the colonel general's current program that would interest Americans except his chaperoning of the Van Dhoc-Da Loc revenge project. Kocho was to store in his memory one final impression of the man. When the time came for Dhoc to return to the helicopter, Kocho saw him do one odd thing: he knelt down for at least a minute in the sand next to the body and the old man could see his lips were moving. Either he was saying a prayer or uttering an oath. Then the tall Vietnamese went back to the helicopter and it took off and flew north on its return journey to Scutari.

30

THE APARTMENT SPANNED THE second floors of three houses down one side of a narrow street. Jakova had pulled the truck to the curb outside a cement staircase that led to the first-floor entrance. There were few people around and they didn't seem curious when Skendi, Pilo, Leeming and the others got out, unloaded suitcases and climbed the stairs. Jakova had told Leeming that the owner of the apartment, Lleshi, was an antiquities smuggler, and there was a mystery as to his whereabouts. Three months ago he'd left his wife and gone into the mountains on his business. Since then, nothing had been heard of him. Jakova thought it was possible Lleshi had been caught by a border patrol

Lleshi's wife opened the door. Jakova's first question was whether her husband had reappeared. The woman looked scared but shrugged off the question saying that her husband was probably enjoying himself in Athens or Crete. Jakova's opinion, quietly delivered to Leeming, was that the woman probably didn't want to face the most likely explanation of what had happened to her husband.

They were shown through the meandering apartment. Although the corridors were long there were few rooms. Jakova allotted one to Skendi and said that he and the others would share one of the large bedrooms. Jakova had told Lleshi's wife they were here to negotiate the purchase of some valuable antiques and their presence must be kept quiet. She would be paid a sum in gold for lodging them.

She had a huge steel pot of coffee ready on their arrival. As they drank, the rain stopped and the late afternoon sky divided into clumps of white puff-cotton clouds. Afterward Leeming suggested they walk to the Scutari citadel.

The rain had been replaced by a cold wind coming down from the mountains. They increased their speed to keep warm. Leeming wondered about the others who had marched up this hill throughout history—Romans, Byzantines, Venetians, Turks, Italians, Nazis. The Scutari citadel had proved the tombstone for the ambitions of many armies. Leeming could not recall any other building that presented such an effect of gloom and dread.

At one point during their walk there, Leeming's eyes met Skendi's and she looked away. He interpreted the movement as acknowledgment that the basis of trust between them had gone. It was true. He could no longer rely on her. He could only use her and she knew it.

The road wound up and ended in a parking lot. There were two buses there, one empty, one filling with tourists. About a hundred people were moving in small groups up and down the main-entrance stairs to the citadel, their cameras shooting the black walls. Leeming let Jakova lead up the wide stone steps.

The fortress was entered by three doorways with immense iron-studded timber doors at least a foot thick. Behind the first door through the massive wall there was an open area. Once houses had been built on this site. But this was the part of the citadel razed by the Turkish conquest and not subsequently rebuilt. They moved across the flattened stone and rubble to the next wall. Above this archway was carved the crescent and star of the victors, above that the Venetian lion of the original builders. Just through the archway on the other side, Leeming saw a vizier's coat of arms cut into the stone.

In this second area a mosque had been erected on the

foundations of a Christian church. Grouped around the mosque were some ancient Christian and Turkish buildings, all of a nondomestic nature, storehouses, granaries, or the ruins of some water cisterns. Leeming looked into the half-dozen buildings alongside the mosque and saw neon-lighted rooms filled with office equipment and steel desks that looked oddly out of place.

They moved through the final archway into the fortress itself. It was obvious that when the Venetians originally purchased Scutari, they had decided that sieges might be a permanent feature and the inner fort should be a building of grandeur and elegance. All the stairs and balustrades were beautifully carved. They climbed up three flights to the battlements.

It hadn't looked so precipitous from the ground, but Leeming now realized he was over six hundred feet above the town below.

"Look," Jakova said suddenly.

But Leeming had already spotted them, three Chinese tourists, at the far end of the battlements. Mackerras had told him there were thought to be over two thousand Chinese technicians in Albania—it seemed reasonable some of them could turn up on a tour of a national monument. On the other hand, this was where Dhoc was hiding out.

"Should we follow them?" Jakova asked. The Chinese had walked off down a staircase.

"No," Leeming said. "Let's check the place. How many rooms here, how many in the rest of the citadel?"

"Maybe fifty rooms in various buildings. Maybe half of them here in the fortress."

Leeming started to tour down the three floors of the fortress, checking through the elegant empty rooms. Although certain doors were locked, all three floors and the dungeons were accessible. Jakova found a notice board which announced that the Scutari fortress would be closing for the night in another half-hour. There were plenty of tourists in the building, but they were collected mainly in the areas of most interest, like the harem quarters on the second floor.

Leeming proceeded down the stone stairs to the ground floor, and crossed into the great hall. This, Jakova said, had been the Venetian officers' mess and banqueting hall. Here the officers had drunk the local wine, planned their forays out to attack the Turks. Here too they had faced the reality of history in 1479 and signed the treaties of defeat. The Turks took everything but spared their lives. Shortly after that victory the Turks introduced a modification to a room beyond the hall. It had probably been a kitchen. They had changed it into a place of execution. Leeming stood with the other tourists and looked through the open door into the room beyond. In the room, high up on the wall, were six huge hooks which had been used for impaling the condemned. The vizier had designed this so that he could sit in the banqueting room in his fine silks, on the richest Kossova carpets, eating his way through huge spiced meals and witness his enemies dying.

Leeming's eyes studied the hooks. They'd hung on that wall for four hundred years. They still glinted dully and he wondered why no one had been sufficiently offended during four hundred years to order them torn out of the wall. Perhaps those in power over the years had felt that their practicability might not yet be over. He could imagine the Nazi occupiers looking up at them forty years ago, minds working their own psychopathic speculations.

Leeming and the others left by a side door and went back outdoors. It was six-fifteen. Nightfall was half an hour away. He was interested that at this time there were still about a hundred men, with their bulldozers and excavation equipment and trucks, working away on the long slopes below.

Jakova had joined a small group listening to a guide. Skendi and Pilo now overtook him. About fifty yards down the sharp slope from the fortress walls they came across the first of several dozen underground water storage cisterns. In former times it had been roofed across the top.

Jakova said the whole of the half-mile-long fortress was built over a rabbit warren of underground viaducts, secret caves and galleries, some containing important burial grounds and other historic treasures hidden and forgotten over the two-thousand-year history of this site. So valuable had been some of the antiquities found here, that in the last three years the government had formed a special department to supervise archeological exploration. Jakova had heard that occasionally the diggings employed over two hundred people. The reason Jakova seemed to have more information than the guide was that he had already benefited from exporting some extremely important Byzantine earthenware stolen from this site.

The half-square-mile area of the current excavations running from three hundred yards below the walls of the south side of the fortress looked like a prisoner-of-war camp. Ten-foot-high wire fencing crowned with barbed wire ran around the perimeter of the site. There was one entrance only, complete with a guardhouse and tall floodlighted gates. Leeming could also see high steel posts with floodlights positioned along the length of the wire.

Jakova continued quietly giving what information he had. There were hundreds of caves and galleries, both natural and manmade, going down to depths of five hundred feet below the citadel. It was also believed that the deeper the archeologists descended, the more ancient the treasures they would find. Jakova added there was a purely commercial motive behind all this. The Albanian government was quietly selling these antiquities, for valued foreign currency, to the West.

In the center of the site there were about thirty long wooden huts, a village larger than the one contained inside the Scutari fortress. Leeming asked Jakova if the site workers lived in these huts. Jakova shook his head saying the huts probably contained the equipment for the complicated skimming process used in digging.

The group and the guide which Skendi and Pilo had attached themselves to now turned around and headed back for the fortress. Leeming stood for a moment longer with Jakova and pondered the task. All those huts down there, plus a citadel with half of its rooms locked up, and numerous underground caves. It would be a needle-in-the-haystack job to locate Van Dhoc.

31

BACK AT THE LLESHI apartment, Leeming set up the
radio and called Paris.

"Marauder A in map ref 407, report reception and
signal." He pressed the receiver button.

He heard Mackerras's voice through the static and
was surprised that after four days Mackerras would still
make himself available for a seven P.M. transmission.

"Marauder B, access signal reception, one hundred
and one hundred. Over."

"Marauder A. Contact established Target B. Infosit,
Target B detailed Target A's reference 407. We are
here, fair attitude though Target B an unplanned terminate." Leeming translated the message that they had
kidnapped Kellezi, who'd pointed them to Van Dhoc at
Scutari, but had then been accidentally a "terminate,"
killed.

"Do I read Target B, repeat B, a terminate?" Mackerras checked that there was no slip. "Target A, Dhoc,
was supposed to be the terminate."

"Positive and regret."

"Explain."

"Too long explanation. Revenge motive of group
member."

"Where is Target A in reference 407?"

"Main town. A citadel."

"Describe, uncoded."

"Scutari citadel, large conglomerate of buildings, of-

165

fices in modern use. A well-known monument. There
will be literature on this building."

"Inspected?"

"Checked once. Very extensive buildings and square-
mile excavations in grounds."

"Explain excavations."

"Massive. Visible work force maybe a hundred. Scutari archeological products major sales to West. A problem that Target B imprecise in locating Target A. Further, this is tourist HQ. Three Chinese visitors
identified. For us expect longtime element in area of ref
407."

There was a pause and Leeming thought that he had
lost Mackerras, but then the general said, "If Target A
is there, I order and require your careful investigation
of this area, citadel and excavations. A description top
detailed for transmit this hour plus twenty-four. Acknowledge."

Leeming pondered whether the order was in any way
at odds with his own plan. It wasn't. "Accord," he said.

"Any requirements?"

"Negative."

"What's your assessment of completion?"

Leeming didn't hesitate. "This terminate on Target
B, if it's ever discovered, will blow the whole thing. I
have poor expectations of a find and hit on Target A,
but equally this will not curb my determined efforts."

Mackerras paused again. Then he said, "You know
why you're doing this, Leeming, better than anyone.
Give me, tomorrow, precisest on the Scutari installations. If Target A is inside there, maybe Buckman and I
can think up something new to pull him out. Add?"

"No."

"Hear you plus twenty-four hours."

"Accord and out."

Leeming switched off the transmit button, dismantled
the radio, sat back and considered Mackerras's order
for a complete physical check on the citadel and work-

ings at Scutari. He thought about the general's observation, that he had the best reason in the world to go on. The general had been wrong about a lot of things, but he was right about that.

32

THE RAIN STARTED AGAIN that night, not heavily, but an intermittent drizzle. Leeming and Jakova hurried through their dinner and set off, the truck banging and grating up the half-macadamed, half-cobbled, streets toward the citadel. The gaunt stone north silhouette was floodlighted, the intention to make the monument look more attractive, but all it achieved was to pinpoint the neglect of the structure, and the garbage left by picnickers—tin cans, broken bottles and plastic packaging. The bright light also nearly disguised the fact there was a number of windows—maybe thirty to forty—on this facade which were themselves lighted. Leeming wondered if anyone was working at this time of night.

They turned right at the east end of the road and drove through the trees to the wire fence around the diggings where Jakova braked, blinded for the moment by the two banks of floodlights on each side of the guardhouse by the main gates. The guardroom door opened and two men stepped out and glared in their direction. Leeming made gestures to Jakova that would be appropriate for someone saying to a driver that he'd come the wrong way. Jakova revved the truck around in reverse. Leeming told him to hurry. He'd seen a telephone on the wall of the hut. He didn't want a call to the police about two late-night explorers on the access road to the Scutari diggings. As the truck turned, Leeming saw that the road wasn't in fact a cul-de-sac. It continued off to the left.

They were halfway back when Leeming ordered Jakova to slow. He'd seen something none of them had spotted from the fortress this afternoon. It was a single railway line. It came out of a tunnel underneath the new road, and wound on another three hundred yards to disappear into an opening in the first steep rise in the foothill foundations of the citadel. The huts had also screened the view of a railway car standing on the line.

Moonlight illuminated its side. There were two spherical steel carboys mounted on it, half hidden by white cladding on which had been painted a black skull-and-crossbones and the word *"Rreziku,"* which Jakova translated as "Danger." Next to that was the legend *"Laget Ajri"*—"Liquid Oxygen." Leeming was about to speculate as to why a liquid oxygen truck should be at an archeological dig, when Jakova offered an answer. Oxygen was necessary for steel welding. If the workmen on the diggings were tunneling through old caves and earthworks, they were probably using welded-steel pit props.

They left the site and headed north toward Tropoja, a town at the foot of a main northern pass, already shut tight at ten o'clock at night. Leeming was familiarizing himself with the physical features of the country, and thinking of the task ahead. They would have to bring the Skoda cars from Tiranha as the truck was now bitterly demonstrating its infirmities. Leeming told Jakova they would have to change their residence before carrying out the initiative. The locus now was the Scutari citadel—the Lleshi apartment was too close to target.

"We'll organize that as quickly as possible," Leeming told him. "Because we're going to make the strike soon, within hours. And when the lights go up on this one it'll be like a kid's thrown a match into a fireworks box. We'll only survive if we've thought out every single move in advance."

Around seven A.M. Jakova and the four men went off on the train to Tiranha to collect the cars. Leeming and Skendi had breakfast—coffee, black bread and a salad of chopped potatoes and radishes in oil. It was a long and silent meal. They were waiting for the hours to pass until the citadel opened at ten A.M.

At nine-forty they walked through the workers forming into bus queues by the long black walls. A weak morning sun, after two days of rain, had already brought out crowds of tourists. At ten, the massive gates were hauled open and the throng filed inside.

She was with him because he'd need someone to talk Albanian if something went wrong and because he was a little worried that she might disappear after the row.

The argument had started almost at midnight. Pilo, the good-looking boy whose manners had seemed milder than the others, had gotten drunk on *raki* and had suddenly started shouting at Skendi, yelling that if she hadn't shot Kellezi the man could have pinpointed the precise whereabouts of Dhoc in the citadel. They could then have killed him, and disappeared fast. She had ruined everything—and worse was probably still to come. They were all bound to be caught. He began to detail what would happen to them when they were apprehended. Skendi had tried to defend herself for half an hour, then given up. She'd gotten up, her eyes filled with tears, and run from the room just as the Lleshi woman, roused from her sleep, came into the living room. No one had gone after Skendi to comfort her. No one had spoken to her that morning.

In 'Nam Leeming had had a one-to-ten quota of women instructors in the Special Forces Camp. He'd had no trouble getting used to the idea of women being around in war. And no reservations. He'd seen them perform equally with men on all occasions. Under pressures of command, like the Tet offensive, he'd shouted at them like he'd shouted at anyone else. He did not consider for a moment that women deserved special treatment. As far as he was concerned, his sympathies were with Pilo.

So he felt cool toward her as he followed her across the yard toward the second archway. She had suckered all of them. It was obvious she'd only joined the group for personal revenge. But now the shoe was on the other foot. Leeming had already had an uncomfortable feeling that he had not kicked her out because he had already decided how best to exploit her. But first he had to work out where in this fortress Van Dhoc would have decided to hide. He was interested in the railway line disappearing below the foundations into the caves as well as in the couple of dozen locked rooms.

Skendi's long stride had put her in front of the tourists just entering the fortress. Leeming caught up to her and indicated with an index finger pointed upward that he wanted to take to the stairs and climb to the upper battlements again.

He was breathing hard by the time they reached the top. She was not. They moved down the narrow guardway between the stone castellations and around to the south side with its view over the excavations. The sun had improved visibility. He could now see the ten-mile extent of the basin around Scutari, the ring of hills on all sides and the mountains to the east.

He studied the diggings again. Workmen were still coming onto the site. Already he could see between sixty and eighty men. He also confirmed that the railway line and car were not visible from the walkway on the south side of the ramparts. He signaled Skendi to precede him. She took to the stairs at the east end of the walkway and they went down to the great hall.

It was there that he saw the two Chinese tourists. He tapped Skendi on the shoulder and signaled she should wait. He followed the two fifty-year-old Chinese through a low archway and walked cautiously to the end of a poorly lighted corridor which ended in a stone spiral stairs leading down. Leeming hesitated. The Chinese tourists were going underground.

Quietly he crept after them but when he reached the bottom they had disappeared. He decided this section of the fortress wasn't open to the public—it didn't seem to be adequately lighted. He also felt a door might open and someone step out and ask him a question in Albanian. He went back up the stairs to Skendi and they walked outside to the terrace containing the exposed water cisterns. Leeming's eyes casually flicked over the workmen, coming back a couple of times to the compound in the middle of the dig, and its huts screening the railway line. That could be Van Dhoc's choice—one of those screened and guarded huts. It was the first and logical step, to search the digs and the thirty huts. That was his decision. Then he wondered why he'd made it and realized the reason was because it was the only one on his list that was possible.

They spent another hour wandering around the exterior of the diggings and then went back to the car and drove to the apartment. The Lleshi woman was out. Skendi made coffee, though Leeming had consumed plenty at breakfast. As she served him he realized she was trying to get up the courage to say something. When she finally spoke, he knew she must have gone to Jakova to learn the English words. "I am sorry," she said. "I am sorry."

He knew he should not make the obvious mistake, attempt to rebuild the bridge that had joined them in her little apartment. He felt it would be an error to release and unbalance emotions now, to reach across and take her hand, to be tempted by an hour stolen for themselves in the empty Lleshi house.

He sat and nodded to her that he understood the words she'd spoken. And then he sensed she too understood there was no going back. She went out to the kitchen and returned a moment later with a raffia shopping basket, indicating she was going out. He nodded. She walked to the door.

"I forgive you," Leeming said gently.

She turned and looked at him for a moment sadly, not knowing the meaning of his words. Then she nodded slowly and went out.

An hour after the girl had gone Jakova returned. As soon as Leeming saw the man's face he knew something had gone badly wrong.

"Kellezi's body's been found. Headlines." Jakova

threw the paper down on the coffee table in front of Leeming.

"How could he have been discovered? I buried him."

Jakova took up the paper and translated the lead story, describing how Colonel General Kellezi, head of State Internal Security, had been tragically killed in a road accident on the sea road near the Kep Palit beach. The car in which he had been driving alone had left the road, gone over a low cliff and smashed on rocks below. He'd died half an hour after admittance to the hospital in Tiranha.

That was the newspaper story. The real story had been told to Jakova by one of Skendi's cousins, Manoe, who'd received a phone call from Kocho. He told them how the dying dog had dug up Kellezi's body, how dozens of police and politicians had arrived and questioned him, and how they had talked about bullets from a new American gun, and how a Chinese man had been flown to the scene by helicopter. He was soft-spoken and tall, just under six feet.

Leeming was silent for a long moment, trying to work out all the combinations of facts. But there was only one conclusion. "I wonder if Van Dhoc assumes Kellezi pointed us to the Scutari citadel?"

"I'm certain he does," said Jakova. "In fact, I see little point in going on to commit suicide."

Leeming gave him a frozen look. "Ever since the girl you selected killed Kellezi I've been waiting for you to take a coward's way out."

Jakova stood quavering. When he was sure he had his temper under control, he hissed, "Never again call me a coward or I will kill you immediately."

Leeming's voice was calculating. "We're here to kill Van Dhoc. Are you with me, yes or no?"

"I, and the others, do not run away. We gave our word."

"This afternoon we find another base," Leeming said flatly. "Tonight you and I are to cut through the wire and explore those diggings. That's my plan. Yes or no?"

Jakova sat down in a chair as if his fury had weakened him and he needed a rest. "You have your answer. Yes."

The anger died quickly. Jakova had made his commitment. Skendi returned from her shopping expedition and Jakova showed her the newspaper. She received all the news in silence, her face expressionless. Jakova told Leeming he didn't think there'd be any problem finding a new place and he went off with Cerrik.

At five he was back. The weather had gotten worse again. The cold watery afternoon sunlight had made way for some black clouds moving in from the mountains. They took the truck, because they were going to have to hide the equipment in the smuggling compartment beneath the rear floorboards. They moved the baggage down and loaded the vehicle. It was six o'clock and starting to rain hard when they finally took the route up past the citadel. Jakova halted for a moment to see where certain strings of traffic pinpointed the roadblocks. There was no way they were going to get out of Scutari without going through at least one police check, but he thought if he drove due north, then west, and north again, they could get out of the town with just one search at the Masi bridge. They moved circuitously down the back streets and finally met the slow-moving crawl of cars heading for the bridge. It took an hour for the truck to filter up to the ten policemen standing at the entrance. The overheating engine was beginning to slow into a series of thumps and jarring backfires.

Leeming was noting what was happening to the cars in front. Each vehicle was stopped, the occupants ordered out at gun-point. The cars' trunks and interiors were searched and the occupants questioned. The process took around three minutes per car.

When it was their turn four officers ordered all of them out of the truck. One of the officials began searching while the captain came across and addressed his first question to Leeming. Jakova stepped in. This was his cousin who was deaf. He couldn't answer any questions but he, Jakova, would answer for him. After a minute, the man at the back of the truck signaled they'd found nothing. The captain, still looking at Leeming, asked Jakova where he had come from, where was he going? Jakova replied that for the fourth time today he was delighted to inform the police that he was going back to his farm at Jezerce having made four journeys with his cousins and some comrade workers to deliver potatoes for the Scutari market. The captain said nothing, still eyeing Leeming. Jakova broke the impasse by simply turning around, climbing back into the truck and pressing the starter. For ten seconds the engine wouldn't turn over. Then it caught, and suddenly the captain was gesturing urgently to Leeming and the others to get back into the truck—perhaps thinking that if the truck stalled again the police might be stuck with the problem of getting rid of it.

Everyone got quickly back on board. With a thump Jakova engaged the gear and the vehicle rattled off across the bridge.

33

LEEMING RECKONED IT WAS eleven miles from Scutari to the new HQ. The journey took an hour and three quarters. Jakova pointed the truck off the Jezerce road and indicated the large ruin among the trees. Jakova explained it was a disused farmhouse. As they drove into the covered courtyard Leeming saw an excellent reason for Jakova's choice. The yard hid the transport. The truck could not be seen from the road or from the air. Equally important, it was within half a mile of the Scutari Agricultural College, providing Leeming with a populated building from which he could bounce his radio transmission.

The farmhouse was on two floors, with a collapsed half-third floor at the east end of the building. Cerrik found a cellar at the west end of the house racked with wine-storage bins. He broke off some rotting wood and quickly had a fire going in a smaller room to the right of the courtyard. This they would use as the assembly room.

While Leeming assembled the radio transmitter, the others secreted the equipment, monoculars, gelignite and akracord fuse, and the M40 rifles in a pile of rubble they found in a corner of the room. Meanwhile Skendi heated up some Turkish coffee, and when it was hot, poured it in paper cups. Leeming studied them. All of them were immersed in a pall of nervousness. This was some kind of watershed. It was as if the risks had suddenly been clarified and the first really serious doubts flowed from them.

Leeming took the radio transmitter and a torch and found a room with a window ledge. He called Paris and told Mackerras what he'd found at the citadel, and of the discovery of Kellezi's body. Mackerras had little to say except that he now wished Leeming to make twelve-hourly contact. Leeming signed off by saying he would.

He returned to the unhappy-looking group and sat down with them by the fire. He felt himself more and more out of sympathy. Here were people who lived by theft. They were all well used to risking their lives.

He waited till midnight, when they had all started to bed down, before signaling Jakova that it was time to go. The roadblock was still operating at the Masi bridge, but the police quickly waved them on. Obviously as the weather had worsened, the rules had slackened.

The Scutari citadel seemed to rear out of the night as lightning flared over it. Leeming ordered Jakova to drive the car right up the road to near the car park. They got out and strode quickly down the wet grass slopes of the southern elevation. Leeming slowed and gestured to Jakova, who'd slowed as well, to take more care as they approached the floodlights. Jakova, his head covered with a black oilskin cap flapping in the wind, made a grunting noise as they moved forward to the shelter of a heavy privet hedge.

The perimeter wire was ten feet away. As far as Leeming could see, the fence was perfectly illuminated—not a shadow to steal into, no dud floodlamp, no obstacle to use as cover.

He looked at Jakova, who shrugged. Leeming pulled out the wirecutters he had thought of abandoning at the airport in Melun. No one around—not a movement anywhere in or out of the flare of lights, no sound other than the rain and the wind rattling the wire. There was no other way except to go out under the lights.

Bending low Leeming ran for the wire. He went down flat and waited several seconds to see whether he'd been spotted. There was no shout, no bullet shot. He took the wirecutters in his right hand and lobbed them onto the wire to see if it was electrified. They bounced off and back onto the ground. He took them up again, got into a half-sitting position, and made his first cut. No alarm bells—silence. In less than a minute he'd made an opening large enough to slide through. He turned to wave to Jakova, but found the man had sprinted the distance and was down on his hands and knees following with Leeming's Smith and Wesson .380 in his right hand. Leeming pulled a couple of strands of the wire back into place and anchored them. Both men got up now and ran for the nearest cover.

It was a dump truck, its bed still filled with rubble. They moved into its shadow and looked back at the fence. Leeming felt the flap cut in it wouldn't be spotted except by someone approaching as close as five yards. He turned and gazed across the dark acres of excavation toward the cluster of long huts. He could now distinguish lights on inside them. Nothing had changed on the site since their predusk view of it, except that the excavators, heavy-duty bulldozers, had been lined up in a file to the right of the huts. Leeming decided to approach the huts from the right, using the vehicles as cover.

He signaled to Jakova and had just started to spring when lightning forked a white sheet across the sky, thunder a second's pause on its tail. Anyone outside on the campsite could have seen them, but again they were lucky. Leeming spotted a giant bulldozer parked fifty yards down the line. This bulldozer had a driver's covered cab sitting fifteen feet in the air atop its superstructure. He reckoned that from there he might get a view down through one of the skylights in the huts.

He told Jakova what he was going to do and moved off. Jakova indicated with his hand he would walk over to check the huts. Leeming made his way down the line of vehicles, reached the giant bulldozer, and started up the steel ladder to the high driver's cab. At the top he pulled open a door and stepped inside.

Lightning flashed again. He saw the complex of hydraulic levers and electric switches for operating the giant machine. The controls of the rig went right around the cab and in order to get to the front of the cab to look down over the nearest hut, he had to climb across the fascia panel. He took a torch from the soaking pocket of his greatcoat, shielding its beam as he switched it on. Through the skylight below him he saw the top halves of two men, guards he assumed, in blue uniforms, playing cards at a table close to the wall, ignoring a small TV security monitor mounted on a bracket above them. Then he saw Jakova moving through the rain down the side of the left-hand group of huts.

Suddenly there was another lightning flash, followed by thunder, immediately followed by the clanging of alarm bells. It was as if the three items were directly linked. Then every floodlight around the compound went on.

Three police cars came racing into the camp followed by a black truck blasting its horn. Leeming saw Jakova dive for the shadows between two huts as a dozen doors opened and people poured out. Half of them were in nightclothes, the others in dungarees or blue uniforms.

The cars and the truck raced to the middle of the compound and skidded to a halt. Doors opened, plainclothes *Shteti Policiza* and two dozen uniformed men, all carrying carbines, jumped out. Cutting the fence wire must have sent a silent signal to police headquarters in Scutari. Almost immediately below him now the men were organizing themselves, shouting above the alarm for the people to get back inside their huts. Their intentions were obvious—to clear the site, then make a systematic search.

He saw several men move forward to collect four German shepherds from the truck. Suddenly the alarm bells were switched off. Then Leeming heard another noise. He turned and stared at the mouth of the tunnel where the single railway line disappeared into the foundations of the fortress. The opening was floodlighted and he could see around twenty people who had walked out and were now standing by the liquid oxygen wagon. At least ten of the twenty were Chinese. Leeming's eyes went over the sallow faces. Suddenly his heart missed a beat. Another man had come up from the darkness of the tunnel. Van Dhoc. If Leeming had had a gun the North Vietnamese captain might be dying now. But he had given the Smith and Wesson .380 to Jakova. He had nothing, not even a penknife.

Or did he? There was the bulldozer itself. He looked from the control panel to where Van Dhoc had stood, but the Vietnamese had gone, presumably back into the tunnel to his quarters deep in the foundations of the citadel. Leeming decided he had better try to escape. He turned the large key in the ignition sequence, heard the clatter fifteen feet below as the electric servos turned over the diesel. For one second he saw confused faces turn. The bulldozer was already lined up so that its forward path would make it collide with at least three of the eight floodlights. He pushed the hydraulic selector into first and pulled back the accelerator. He didn't need to know where he was going in order to make a judgment about when the maximum damage had been done. He felt the giant machine shake. His ears were deafened by the accelerating howl of the diesels as the bulldozer, its huge ramp at half mast, set off, accompanied by the shouts of the soldiers, the howls of the dogs and the bark of gunfire. It first hit an empty police car, then went on to smash down the three-in-line floodlights which collapsed in sparks of arcing short circuits. And on, this time to the sound of human screams as it reached the first hut and crushed through it, shredding its timbers like matchwood. And then suddenly in the shuddering insides of the cab, it was dark. He leaped across the bucking floor and grabbed the access ladder and was scaling down, the machine still grinding its own route across the pitch-black workings of the site. He slid on the wet rungs and was thrown onto the mud. He got up fast, sprinting flat-out across the pockmarked excavations, heading up toward the gap in the fence.

He reached the wire, heard running footsteps behind him, turned, and saw Jakova bolting up the last yards, the steel glint of revolver in his hands.

"Shoot." Leeming pointed. Jakova aimed for the two nearest floodlights and fired twice. They went out. In the half-darkness they pulled themselves through the gap in the wire and then were running again, up the steep inclines of mud, wet stone and slippery grass, heading for the citadel walls. If they had paused a second to turn they would have seen there was no immediate pursuit—the policemen had plenty to do handling the huge bulldozer. It had cut through three huts, then the tracks on the right hand of the vehicle had fallen into a deep ditch which went in a half-circle. The effect was to steer the machine around and out of the ditch and off on a new path of destruction. It had reached the south line of the fence, torn it down and disappeared out of view into a field pursued by a dozen running men.

They jogged back to the Skoda and Jakova drove off into the night streets of Scutari, meeting little traffic on the road. When they reached the Masi bridge the guards had gone, evidently summoned to help in the crisis at the dig. They didn't see any police as they left town, but they heard several horns moving fast to the area of the citadel.

34

IT WAS TWO A.M., and the rain was fading. Leeming sat back in the rattling truck and tried to draw up a kind of balance sheet. They'd escaped. He'd located his quarry, but at what price? The security at the diggings was bound to become tighter after tonight's incident. On top of that he was convinced that the final hunt for Van Dhoc must be initiated within hours.

They got back to the farmhouse and found Cerrik on guard—the rest asleep. Cerrik reheated the coffee for the three of them. And then Leeming and Jakova laid out blankets on the floor and went to sleep. Leeming gave orders, through Jakova, that he was to be wakened at eight A.M.

As soon as he was up, Leeming radioed Paris. The general's voice came on the line as if he'd been up for several hours.

"Marauder One, we have your top signal strength, over."

"Marauder Two, this is Marauder One. This transmit to your order. Give me your message or instructions over."

"Marauder One, how are you fixed?"

"We have made definite ID on Target A at referred diggings."

"Are you sure?" Mackerras' voice sounded pleased, as if he'd done it all himself.

"Positive. Initiative imminent now."

"Whereabouts in the dig? Exact location?"

Leeming wasn't sure why Mackerras would want that information. "Previously described railway line, the liquid oxygen truck. Railway line goes into foundations. Believe target in quarters under citadel."

"Copy. Now attention to this. I have sent Buckman to you. Flew coop here 2200 ETA your area map reference 404F landed 0530 confirmed. He has come to help you."

At first Leeming couldn't believe he had heard correctly. He was stunned. "Marauder Two on hold," he said.

He reached into a pocket, took out the project map and spread it out on the window ledge. He traced reference 404F. It seemed to be a belt of woods about ten miles north of the farmhouse. "Marauder Two, what the hell is Buckman here for?" Leeming was angry now. "Supposing he's picked up? He has total information in the event of successful interrogation. What do we need Buckman for?"

Silence from Mackerras for a moment, and then a low-voiced cold retort. "Don't worry, Colonel, he ain't going to make you pogie-bait." Mackerras used the U.S. soldiers' Vietnam slang for gun fodder. "Your carriage not A-one so far. You need Buckman. Go to 404F. It's a small wood. Southeast corner, from our input, there's an unmanned electricity substation. He'll meet you there. Now get this clear. I approve Buckman's joint command with you. You work it out with him. My reckoning, that's the only way you'll make Target A." The general signed off.

Leeming still couldn't work it out. What was the meaning, and why the immediacy with which this had happened? Buckman in Albania, "confirmed," Mackerras had said, ten miles up the road. Why send him? Why split command decisions? He felt a sense of hopelessness, then controlled it. Buckman was not going to give him the run-around.

The journey into the mountains took little time. The roads were almost empty. Jakova explained most of the farmers would be in Scutari for market day. When they finally reached the box reference 404F on the map, Leeming could see why the site had been chosen for the Feiseler landing. It was ringed by radar-defeating high mountains. Access to the valley was by a series of S-bends in the road. The journey down through these bends took the best part of half an hour. Anyone in the wood would be able to hear approaching traffic with plenty of time to hide.

The substation was a windowless cement structure bristling with pylons and ceramic terminals. It was the only building in the forest and stood alongside the Jezerce road. There was no other traffic in sight. Jakova drove past the building, stopped the truck, drove back and halted.

A minute passed. No movement. Then Buckman stepped out from behind some wild olive trees and started walking toward them. He was dressed in torn dungarees, a blue donkey jacket and carried a large carpenter's tool bag. His hair had been cut close to his skull. Leeming got down from the truck and went to meet him. Buckman extended his hand. Leeming shook it perfunctorily.

"Morning."

"I'm expecting a full and satisfactory explanation for your arrival here," Leeming said.

"I've come to help get Van Dhoc."

"What can you contribute?"

"The general thinks you've been taking a helluva time to get this project together." Buckman lifted himself inside the cab and shook Jakova's hand.

Leeming climbed up and sat alongside Buckman. He would say nothing for the moment, because he was sure the man had not come to Albania for the reason he and Mackerras had given.

Back at the farmhouse, the Albanians studied Buckman, intimidated enough by his presence to be thoughtful, not questioning. He'd eaten breakfast with the rest of them, enthusiastically. Pasta, and a ground meat dish spiced and colored deep red with paprika. It was eleven

A.M. The skies had cleared again, the winds had gone, but the air was cold.

Leeming made an introduction speech. Buckman was an experienced U.S. Army colonel who'd come to help. He gave details of the man's history—West Point, GHQ posting as an Intelligence expert in Saigon. Buckman prodded him on with tidbits of self-information. The others listened puzzled as they ate their food. Maybe something had communicated itself, Leeming thought, between himself and the group—the real question— what was the man here for?

Skendi waited until the introduction was over. She spoke and Jakova translated.

"She asks," Jakova addressed Buckman, "what particular aid can you give us?"

Buckman looked businesslike. "I brought something with me. In the circumstances it might prove very effective." He put down his plate, crossed the room to the table where he had placed the mud-covered tool bag, and brought it back to the center of the room. He unzipped it and started to pull out and assemble sections of an M47 grenade launcher. It took him four minutes to snap and bolt the various sections together. He handed it to Jakova. He then pulled out a green fiberglass box and opened it. There were six grenades inside. Buckman turned and faced the group. "Tell them I have heaard from Colonel Leeming and yourself of the incident at the citadel last night. I appreciate the security at the diggings is good. At the same time you and Colonel Leeming got in and out alive. Here's my opinion. I don't believe that the security forces at Scutari will reckon the people who raided the place last night will return in broad daylight this afternoon."

Leeming stopped himself from commenting.

"I believe we can get back inside that wire today. I know that by firing a grenade at that railway wagon of liquid oxygen we'll cause a major explosion. And I've worked out a plan that I guarantee will result in the locating and execution of our quarry Van Dhoc."

Jakova translated. There was silence from the group.

Leeming started to speak.

Buckman held up a cautioning hand. "Now I'll tell you my plan for getting in, pulling the head off this chicken, and getting out."

35

IT WAS FOUR O'CLOCK. Leeming checked the items being loaded into the hidden compartment of the truck. The dismantled M47 with two grenades, the six M40 rifles, Leeming's own Smith and Wesson, two pounds of gelignite, akracord incendiary fuse, monoculars, twenty feet of strong rope. There were only fours hours of daylight left. The pressure was on.

Buckman had spoken well. His plan, as Leeming was first to acknowledge, was excellent. His calculations made back in Mackerras' office at SHAPE were clever, consistent and possible. So much so that Leeming had to consider in all honesty that Mackerras' opinion, couched so crudely—"He thinks you've been taking a helluva time to get this project together"—had perhaps some truth in it. Buckman, with less information than Leeming had about the diggings, had flown in with ideas that had a real chance for getting Van Dhoc out into the open. The plan was elegantly simple. And if something went wrong it didn't suddenly collapse; certain components stood by themselves. Leeming didn't have to suggest the smallest alteration.

The others had sat through Jakova's translation, thoughtful. Their questions had been simply for clarification. If they were to risk their lives, they wanted to be clear on the fine detail. But Leeming could see they also thought the plan would work. Within two, maybe three hours, it would all be over—and they would be traveling north to escape from a political regime which had

mutilated their families and their futures. And they
would have hurt that regime, badly. One by one they
had told Jakova of their agreement.

At midday Jakova had been sent into town with Haziz. They were to take the monocular and find a point
on the east hill overlooking the new road and survey the
site. The operation could not start until Van Dhoc was
positively spotted in the area of the dig. Now Jakova
had returned to tell them Van Dhoc had arrived in a
chauffeur-driven car and had disappeared into the tunnel opening.

They were ready for the last journey to the citadel.

They drove into Scutari and almost into a trap which
had been set at the Lleshi house. They were saved by a
second's coincidence. They arrived down the street from
the house just as a group of six policemen were sprinting up the steps changing guard with another six running out to a truck parked at the curb. Jakova, on an
instinct, had stopped several yards away. The two
Skoda cars that had been brought up from Tiranha
were parked another twenty yards down the street.

Jakova exchanged worried looks with Leeming and
Skendi. Who had betrayed them? But it was too late to
wonder about that now. Leeming decided it was worth
the risk to pick up the closest Skoda. At a word from
Jakova, Cerrik got out of the truck, walked up to the
first car, and drove off.

Jakova waited a moment, engaged gear, and the
truck rattled off up the cobbles.

Leeming took a quick look as they passed the house.
The shutters were open as usual, but maybe in one of
the back rooms they held the woman, and maybe she
had told them already of the visitors, and the American
among them.

They trailed Cerrik up through the late afternoon
town. Five-fifteen P.M. the last of the schoolchildren
and women factory workers were forming long queues
for transport. He could hear the vital sounds of young
voices and wondered in a second's flash of black pessi-

mism whether this would be the last time he heard them. He wondered too about how the last minutes would go, and about the silence his life would leave behind. There would be that Pentagon caller one morning at the door of his brother's farmhouse, giving the bare news and the caution that he'd died performing a sensitive mission for his country. And his brother would take the news quietly, and ask questions, but never enough, and that would be the end of it.

They drove down the avenue of acacias marking the north citadel wall. There was some traffic, a dozen bicyclists, and a bus, a half-dozen cars, the beginning of the evening rush to the suburbs.

Jakova turned the Skoda right at the bottom of the wide street. Leeming felt calm, but was aware of the adrenalin starting to spur the preparations for action along the network of his nerves. He could feel his grip tighten on the butt of the Smith and Wesson in his pocket. He took a sidelong look at Skendi as they turned into the slip road to the diggings and Jakova braked to a halt. She seemed ice-cold, no fear on her face. Jakova was looking out the cab window, seeing no one, and no motor traffic. He turned and looked across Leeming to Skendi, and ordered her out. "*Shkne,* Skendi, *shkne!*"

A fraction's hesitation, enough for a last look at the two of them, and she was gone. Leeming heard the others scrambling out of the rear of the truck—Pilo, Dmitri and Buckman running for the bushes.

Leeming saw three of them—Pilo, Dmitri and Skendi, each carrying an M40, sprint flat-out across the fifty yards of bushes down the gentle drop to near the wire perimeter of the diggings. On the other side of the road Buckman was running in the opposite direction, through more scree and scrub, fifty yards up to the top of the hill where he would assemble the M47 and fire one grenade. But the plan depended on everyone being in position, and a key precise maneuver involving Cerrik's Skoda and the crude bomb.

In the car Cerrik had braked in behind the truck and now followed Jakova and Leeming.

Leeming studied the diggings. Between fifty and sixty people were visible on the site, but there was no sign of guards. The section of fencing which the huge bulldozer had ploughed through had been crudely repaired. Leeming didn't trust the scene below—it all appeared too calm.

It had happened before in 'Nam. He'd be leading a patrol through a night forest and he'd hear the forest go silent, and realize he'd walked into a trap. But there was no turning back. There was to be one final check with Haziz, still sitting it out at the top of the hill studying the railway tunnel entrance with the monocular. Dhoc had gone into the tunnel nearly two hours ago. If he'd come out and left the site, then everything would be called off for today. Otherwise it was on.

If they were heading into a trap, then from the silence it was not yet sprung, and it was only minutes away. And if the first attack succeeded, there would be a sequence, and once started, the enemy would find it impossible to counterattack. Or would they. Did they have a plan that outflanked all the contingencies that their own plan had accounted for?

Jakova reached the bottom of the road and turned sharply left up the rise and turned at the gatehouse. Cerrik followed. Leeming gave the gatehouse a piercing look, but saw no evidence of guards.

There was a further reason for the precisely concentrated look—it was to line up angles. To confirm a calculation that if Cerrik's driverless car, with its steering wheel tied by rope, and accelerator weighted to the floor, and carrying a gelignite bomb in the rear, if that car hit those wire mesh gates it would tear a way through them, and get somewhere near the circle of wooden huts. This part of the plan had to work if the more important part was to fall into place.

The truck, engine protesting, scaled up the two-hundred-yard slope to the top of the hill. Just over the crown, Jakova pulled the vehicle over and braked to a halt. Cerrik in the car followed suit. No other traffic around. No one in sight except Haziz running fast out of a clump of bushes to the left of the road.

Leeming and Jakova got out of the truck fast. Haziz shouted at Jakova as he approached.

"Van Dhoc has not reappeared," Jakova told Leeming.

"Turn the car around and start to rig the gelignite." Leeming pointed to the monocular Haziz was carrying, strung over his shoulder. Haziz pulled it off and gave it to him.

Running as fast as he could Leeming headed down the road and off to the right, into a small olive grove, up another steep slope, then down, toward a small knoll from which he could look down on the area where Buckman was positioning the grenade launcher.

He looked at his watch. It was nearly five-forty. What he wanted to check was whether there was any sign that they had been spotted. Below, the regulated order of movement was unchanged.

He peered down through the monocular. Skendi, Dmitri and Pilo were all secreted away now in the bushes by the wire. But he could see clearly part of Buckman's head and shoulders. Buckman was squatting in the bushes, the grenade launcher assembled, held over his shoulder, the lemon-shaped M47 grenade sticking out of the barrel.

He turned and ran through the olive grove again and sprinted across to Jakova, Cerrik and Haziz who were urgently finishing their preparations with the car and the bomb. It was a primitive bomb, consisting of a two-pound lump of Dow gelignite, still in its plaspak, with a two-foot-long ten-second fuse of phosphorus akracord.

They'd positioned the gelignite package and taped it with adhesive tape to the rear seat on the left side, directly above the car's petrol tank. Leeming checked it with one glance, nodded to Jakova. Jakova took out a box of matches. Meanwhile Cerrik and Haziz made certain the steering wheel was roped tightly into a fixed position. They started maneuvering a stone slab brought, in the truck, from the farmhouse, which was now on the driver's side of the floor. The edge of the heavy slab was pressing down on the accelerator pedal. The engine was revving high and the racket would soon draw someone's attention at the guardhouse.

Leeming took Jakova's matches and struck one, reached in and lighted the end of the akracord fuse. It flared, and started to burn, spitting and sparkling. He nodded to Jakova and the other two who had run to the back of the car. They crouched low and started to push. The door on the driver's side of the Skoda was still open. Leeming bent his shoulder against that, using it as a lever to accelerate the car, the engine still screaming high revs. If the clutch was put in now, engine power would strip it or the gear box. Slowly, under pressure from the four of them, the car moved forward, and then faster, as the momentum took and the vehicle found the gravity of the initial slope that within yards would move it onto the steep fall of the hill.

Leeming jumped into the front seat, pulled the gear lever into third, and braced himself automatically against the jerk. The clutch held, the car was suddenly going at twenty, accelerating to thirty. He threw himself out, a poorly improvised parachute roll, screamed inwardly as one of his knees cracked on the tarmacadam, but a second later he was up and hurtling at full speed toward the man in the uniform who had just appeared over the brow of the hill to investigate. The guard had his carbine slung over his shoulder. He either didn't see Leeming pull out the Smith and Wesson or didn't react fast enough. Leeming fired three times, saw the guard's chest rip open in a mess of cloth and blood, and saw the man fall. Leeming was still running as hard as he could, the others following, along the path that the Skoda had taken.

They halted by some bushes at the crown of the hill. Seconds later the others were alongside him, looking down. But then Jakova and the other two were off and running again, to the right, heading for the olive grove and their new positions.

The driverless Skoda headed straight down the hill. The guards standing outside the guardhouse, drawn by the noise of engine and the gunshots, managed to fire some random shots at the car about a second before it hit the double-wire gates at seventy miles an hour.

It charged on. Twenty yards inside the compound one of its tires hit a rock and shredded, and the whole car somersaulted twice high in the air and collapsed in a heap of disintegrating metal and bursting glass near the center of the wooden-hut compound. The bomb went off—first a single detonation, then a second explosion as the full petrol tank of the Skoda blew up. Suddenly there were thirty, forty, fifty men pouring out of the huts, the same critical confusion as last night, the same instant scream of alarm bells and a half-dozen armed security people jumping into two cars, ploughing furrows around and across toward the dismantled gates and the new road outside. Leeming knew these people would be coming to trace who had launched the car. He bent double and ran off toward the right, in the direction of the olive grove, revolver in one hand, monocular in the other. Fifty yards on he could see Haziz charging down now through the high bushes to the new road, his M40 gripped in the firing position.

He reckoned they had ten minutes before the police spilled out of their HQ in town and made it into trucks and cars up to the diggings. Ten minutes to get Skendi, Pilo, Dmitri, Cerrik, himself, in through that wire to kill Van Dhoc when the oxygen flames lighted through the underground diggings and drove everyone in the hidden underbelly of Scutari to the surface.

Leeming had pressed through the grove and duplicated his first trip to the grassy knoll abutment of the hill. He threw himself down flat in the bushes, panned the monocular across, focusing in on the blazing wreckage of the Skoda, and the white-coated men who had run out of the huts and were now shouting orders at the laborers and the bulldozer drivers. Obviously they were organizing them to do exactly what Buckman's plan called for, but with a slight variation, perhaps a fatal variation on the plan.

Buckman had anticipated the men in the diggings would spot the danger of the proximity of the liquid oxygen to the burning car. He'd reckoned they'd rush to get the truck with its explosive load moved away. The railway truck was on a slope and Buckman had thought the release of the truck's handbrake would allow gravity to power it down the ten yards into the wide entrance of the tunnel. As soon as the truck moved into the tunnel, Buckman was to fire the grenade that would puncture and explode the liquid oxygen carboys. The thousand-degree heat and explosion would go two ways, the first way out into the open air, the other down burning into the bowels of the fortress.

Someone must have released the brake lever. Gravity failed to start the truck rolling. Leeming could see sudden activity around a large excavator as a driver turned it around and moved it in to give the railway wagon a push. Then he saw Buckman's unexpected problem. The mass of the bulldozer was now screening the railway wagon as it moved in and push-started the wagon down the track to the tunnel entrance.

In the monocular he saw Buckman getting up and running with the M47 to find a new firing position fifty yards over to the left. He heard more gunfire, pointed the monocular at the road below. More guards had run out through the main gates, had spotted Buckman and were firing at him.

The pall of white smoke coming out of the burning Skoda turned to thick black clouds as the tires started to burn. The smoke was rising to obscure Buckman's view of the tunnel and the bulldozer.

Leeming panned back, saw Buckman fall forward, thought for a second he was shot, then realized he'd reached the last rise of the mount above the road. From here he could get his view of the wagon behind the bulldozer. Buckman levered himself up on an elbow, parted the tall grass with the long barrel of the M47, aimed carefully and fired. The grenade could almost be seen on its horizontal path through the air as it hit and pierced the thick metal of the carboy, which instantly detonated.

Leeming couldn't believe what followed. The grenade traveled the two hundred yards, hit the oxygen carboys, and the first white-heat explosion blew a pall of earth up into the sky. There was a second's pause then a sudden rippling of explosions, half-seconds dividing them, and all louder than the first. And Leeming felt the ground shaking beneath him, and suddenly the sky, up to five hundred feet above the tunnel entrance, blew up. In the last second before he dropped the monocular and ran toward the dust and smoke-fog of the explosion, he saw that Buckman had thrown aside the M47 and was running away from it, and that, when he thought about it later, was the proof that the man knew exactly what was to come, because this was the beginning of a hell of destruction, not the end.

Leeming ran, Smith and Wesson held across his chest, his body slicing through the bushes, down toward the lower road. He'd gone thirty yards when the first of the new blasts hit him, picked him up, spun him around like a top, and threw him flat on his back. Then the heat hit, and he knew this was no ordinary explosion, yet he was up and running again down the slope, sliding, falling, bumping and smashing his way down. Then the second series of explosions came.

The first had blown everything on the surface of the half-mile sprawl of the site up into the air. He could see nothing now except the solid fog, five hundred feet high, of thick brown dust. Yet still he ran on because the group of Skendi, Jakova and the others were dying in the heat down there, sent by himself into the inferno, to be murdered by Buckman. Because suddenly Leeming knew the reason for the plot hatched by Buckman and Mackerras was to kill everything that moved on this site in Albania. And it had nothing to do with Van Dhoc—it could have nothing to do with him.

The third explosion came so fiercely that the brown fog was gone, blown in a ripple of blasts higher into the air. He'd crossed the road and had almost reached the wire when he was flung with the wire fence thirty feet back across the road.

Then an immense detonation pinned him with its blast flat against the horizontal earth embankment on the other side of the road. He saw it all. He saw two huge pairs of concrete doors that had been hidden by the disguise of the archeological dig being blown open, and the remnants of at least five or six ballistic missiles being hurled in a thousand pieces of shredded steel and titanium high into the air. He saw Chinese men covered in blood and flames running, staggering, hauling themselves out of previously hidden tunnel entrances. And as he fought for consciousness he saw for the first time the real identity of the Scutari digs and what the archeological lie had disguised. This was the Chinese government's missile foothold in Europe. In exchange for the support of their economy, the Albanians had allowed the Chinese to build this rocket installation within the short strategic distance of their common enemy, Moscow.

He felt his own blood pouring from wounds in his head. He sensed the near-end of consciousness as he staggered to his feet. Then he collapsed again, his hands going up to protect his head as he saw the largest blast so far rip a four-hundred-foot-wide excavation across the center of the site, like the explosion of a volcano, and the last of the huts were crushed to a million splinters, and the black silhouettes of bodies of burned men were being hurled through the air. Then somewhere, on the east edge of the site, a steel silo with doors covering a hidden helicopter pad, opened, and a helicopter blazing from the stern flew up a hundred feet into the sky, turned on its side and blew apart. And then the heat from this blast hit him, and his body jackknifed in a scream. Just as that happened, the whole middle section of the dig dropped thirty or forty feet with a roar that superceded all the chemical explosions of the underground fuel storage tanks of liquid oxygen and nitrogen. He realized this meant the collapse of the entire steel

skeleton of the galleries that housed the scientists, their
sleeping quarters, the radar and computer rooms, the
control centers and the firing gantries of this top-secret
unheard-of rocket installation. And now he was being
harshly bounced around on the ground, coughing, deep
retching coughs, his lungs full of dust and gasping for
air, but the air had been burned. And the world spun
and he was overcome with the final blackness of nightmare as he realized they would all be dead out there—
Jakova, Cerrik, Pilo, Haziz, Dmitri and Skendi, all
burned to death. Buckman would survive. Buckman
had known the score—had led them into this valley of
death. And he still lived. Leeming surrendered his consciousness on the final borders of pain.

He remembered trying to work out the scale of his
injuries and tried to determine whether his right foot,
slippery with blood inside his shoe, was smashed beyond repair, or just twisted so badly that the pulsing,
jarring pain could compete in intensity with any other
of the broken centers of his body. His spine felt as if it
was smashed but somehow he pulled himself onto his
knees. It was the back of his head—that was the main
source of blood loss. His fingers explored from his neck
up to the crown. There was no skin there—just fresh
blood. The final injury was the burning. He felt he must
have second-degree burns on his hands and face and
that they would throw him into shock.

He didn't know how long it took, but somehow he
was starting to pull himself forward on hands and
knees, and inching up the still-burning grass embankment, choking with the dust and thick smoke. In front
of him, right up the hill, all the bushes and trees were
on fire. He stopped, turned painfully to look back to see
if there was a hope that any of them had lived, but
apart from the lazy drift of a whole sky of smoke, there
was no movement at all on the site. He crawled another
fifteen feet upward and again lost consciousness.

Later he was to realize he had only been unconscious
a minute or so. It seemed like hours until the black cob-
webs broke apart and he saw light again. Paradoxically

the faint had refreshed him, given his body a chance to mobilize itself. He came out of the nightmare and knew he would go on. He would test his final reserves in a last agonizing effort which would either kill or save him.

If he could climb the hill. The truck would still be sitting in the upper road. It would have been shielded from the blast. If he could get to the truck there was a chance.

In the half-world of consciousness and unreality he had mislaid the logical processes that would have told him the task was impossible, his body too injured. But he had too many compulsions to survive. And one in particular. He must send a last message to Mackerras. He must talk to the man who had ordered the mass murder.

Had Buckman survived? He had run, after firing the M47, but at that point he had been nearer to the source of the first explosions than Leeming. Had he already gotten to the truck and driven off in it? Where was he when the main explosions blew everything apart? Why should he have survived? Maybe the man's death was part of Mackerras' plans. No one left alive as a witness.

Leeming started up the slope in a kind of falling-forward motion. He was trying to scream with the pain but he couldn't because he was choking so much. He blacked out twice on the four-hundred-yard journey. The first time his head crashed down on an outcrop of stones. The second time he didn't think he'd make it forward again. A kind of madness powered the determination that got him up the hill. Then for the first time he pulled himself properly upright, and blundered off through the olive grove, aiming himself from one tree to grasp to another. Then he was through it and out of the other side and halting, almost unbelieving. The truck was still there, empty.

Buckman was a hundred yards away, back to him, standing half-hidden in the fog of dust, obviously un-harmed. He started forward again unable to work out what Buckman was doing. And then he saw that he was holding a camera. No doubt waiting for the smoke to clear a little more, to take his pictures, destined for Mackerras' desk. The photographs needed to substantiate his report of success in fooling Leeming and the Albanian group into cooperating fatally and unknowingly in the destruction of the rocket site.

He stumbled down the road, grabbed the tailboard of the truck and steadied himself. Buckman had begun taking photographs. He debated. The other man had not yet seen him. What would happen when he did? Buckman was no ally—he was the enemy. In a minute he'd return to drive the truck away. Would he want Leeming along with him? Hadn't he outlived his usefulness?

He applied his bloody fingers to the hasp that held up the tailgate and tried to pull it out. It took three exhausting attempts, fingers slipping on the metal, before he succeeded in unhooking the tailgate and pulling himself onto the rear platform of the truck and closing the tailgate. He fell forward on the floor in semiconsciousness. It could have been a minute or an hour—suddenly he heard the truck start up, reverse and head off. And then the truck was bumping and jarring each wound in his body, and he blacked out again.

36

HE COULD HEAR A voice. The truck was parked and he was still lying in the back. He could hear bird songs. Turning over, he saw through a gap in the canvas flaps the farmhouse and the swallows flying in and out. He lay still a minute, then tried to flex his arm and leg muscles to get the circulation going again. Slowly he turned from his back onto his front. He reached out, found an upright stanchion on the truck's side, and pulled himself, sick with pain, into a sitting position. Buckman's voice was coming out of the window six feet away. He'd placed the wireless transmitter on the window sill.

"Full hit," Buckman was reporting to Mackerras. "Everything. Underground silos, fuel tanks, hardware, software. An area goddam near a half square mile caved in, dropped thirty feet. The explosions were amazing. I nearly lost it too. Yes, all of them, I'm afraid. Leeming, Jakova and the others. It is to be regretted. Nonetheless they played their part. General, this has to be the greatest G2 initiative in this Army's history. Same reference, 404F. . . . No, I'm just eleven miles from there. Tell Meyer I'll be expecting him behind the power station as soon as it's dark, say 2100 hours. Maybe see you tomorrow. Marauder Three over and out." There was silence.

Leeming called out. "Buckman," the word coming faint across his parched lips. He tried again, this time it was louder. "Buckman!"

He could imagine Buckman standing by the window, dismantling the radio set, suddenly hearing his name, recognizing the voice. He could imagine the man freeze, bewildered. This had not been part of his plan.

Leeming sat back and waited. Ten, twenty seconds passed, and then the flap on the back of the truck was pulled aside.

"How did you get in here?" Buckman asked, his voice flat and dangerous.

He could see the man hesitating, trying to work it out, as if it wasn't a question of a wounded man needing help, but a problem with variable answers.

"How hurt?" he asked.

"Give me your hand."

Buckman seemed to make up his mind, decided for the moment to aid Leeming, if only to give himself time for planning. Leeming knew that to Buckman he must look like a dying man. Face and hands and head awash with fresh blood. But Leeming had determined he wasn't going to die. He was going to survive on the strength of his will to expose and punish. This man and Mackerras had sent them into a trap, asked them to light the touch paper on too short a fuse, and killed them—Skendi, Jakova and the others—with premeditated callousness. Whatever was left of his life now was more strongly motivated toward a goal than in any previous time of his existence.

Buckman pulled down the tailgate and studied him, the expression on his face a mixture of confusion and irritation that he seemed to be trying to stop from expressing in words. He pulled Leeming's legs around and slowly slid his body over the tailgate, out of the truck into a standing position. He then gripped him under the arms and hauled him backward across the cobbles through the open doors of the courtyard and into the farmhouse.

"What'll I do first?" Buckman asked. "Dress the wounds?"

"Something to drink." Leeming moved his limbs around to try to arrange a lessening of the pain. He looked across the room. Buckman had cleared everything away. There was no sign anyone had recently occupied this place except the radio and an M40 carbine leaning against the wall next to the transmitter.

Buckman went to the rear of the room, kicked aside some rubble, came out with Skendi's screw-top tin of coffee. "No water. Cold coffee?"

Leeming nodded.

He came back, opened the cap, and held the tin for Leeming. He drank.

"There's a First Aid box, under the stones."

Buckman returned to the heap of rubble, kicked more earth and stones away with his foot. He found the small black box and brought it back. He opened it and examined the contents. "Morphine?"

Leeming shook his head.

Buckman spilled some bandages on the floor. Then he started to examine Leeming, pushed him gently forward first to trace the main source of fresh blood at the back of his head.

The examination took a couple of minutes. Buckman stood up and pronounced, "Broken foot, ankles both sprained, deep cuts in the head—loss of blood. Second-degree burns. Can you stand?"

"No."

"You'll make it. I've been in contact with Paris. Meyer's coming in, 2100. You relax now, in six hours, we'll be in Italy. I'm going outside to get the truck and bring it into the covered yard, just in case they're scouring the countryside. Though I doubt any survived who could describe us."

"No one survived. No one had time to phone the police. Everybody died." Leeming's voice was almost a croak. "There'll be no pursuit."

Buckman turned. "I'll bring the truck in anyway."

He walked out.

Leeming listened. He supposed the time span was five minutes, maybe a little more. The sound was of the grinding starter of the old truck mixed with Buckman's harsh cursing. He heard the hood going up, then a minute of silence.

He stared at the radio pack sitting on the window ledge. He was unsure whether his body was capable of reaching it but his mind gave the order. He fell forward, let the pain rack through his body, then began to crawl. He nearly blacked out again on the tiny journey, but somehow his will grappled and clung to consciousness. With a final deep shudder of searing pain, he pulled himself around and sat back next to the radio. He heard a shout, almost a scream, then running footsteps and Buckman hurled himself into the room. "Jesus, Leeming, there must be someone outside. Someone's grabbed the rotor cap. The truck won't work. And they've grabbed the wiper blades."

Leeming's heart sank. He wondered if Buckman knew the significance of what he was saying. The man's face was white, probably because of the loss of transport, the route of escape cut.

Leeming's voice came out rasping and low. "Remember the VC before the monsoons? They'd steal into our truck parks, remove rotor caps. It amused us—they'd also steal our wiper blades. They didn't realize how easily we could replace items like that. Wiper blades stolen from a VC truck in the monsoon period meant the truck was inoperable maybe for months until spare blades arrived from the long journey down the Ho Chi Minh trail. Van Dhoc's outside, Buckman. He's here." Leeming's voice was so brittle he was not sure the horrified Buckman could hear him. "Sorry. He can only have one of us. I'm also owed a debt." Leeming leaned over, grasped the M40 and in one movement brought it around and up. He fired. A burst of six shells sliced down the front of Buckman's body with such unexpected recoil that Leeming dropped the gun.

Buckman, flattened against the wall, stood there dead for five seconds, the features of his face locked in a scream of incomprehension before he collapsed slowly forward, first onto his knees and then heavily forward onto his face.

Leeming sat there, fought for his consciousness and the reality of Van Dhoc. He moved into semiconsciousness.

Time started to play games with him, mixing truth and untruth, supporting the bizarre charade of faulted phenomena—was the afternoon moving grayly into evening, or was he simply floating gradually off into final unconsciousness? He knew he was in shock. His whole body would shake for a quarter of an hour, or a minute, or whatever time meant, shake itself into exhaustion. He knew there would be an end to this phase of trauma before it moved into a final deterioration. But that only gave him an acute sense of helplessness. At the other end of this period of shock there would be Van Dhoc.

He started a dream which turned quickly to a nightmare. It was about the city of Hue during the Tet offensive. Hue in February 1968, when orders from MACV (American Forces HQ) had reached Leeming and every other noncombatant officer in the Special Forces Camp, instructing a move to the nearest city center to give all aid in its defense. The first reports of the Tet offensive's massive and unexpected assaults on the major towns of the Delta, like Saigon and Hue, had come in on January 30. By February 5, thirty of the forty-four provincial towns were under attack. Leeming had gone to Hue, had been assigned a forward communications liaison post with a section of the First Cav. He'd arrived on February 1. The day before, the National Liberation Army had entered Hue from the south, seized half a dozen U.S. tanks and virtually overrun the city, first calling at the jails to release three thousand prisoners. They had had a certain amount of organizational help. Professors and students of the university came out openly on the streets on the communist side.

It had been cold when Leeming arrived. He found the First Cav section sitting around fires in the open, confused by gunfire coming from all directions. Even MACV seemed to be uncertain about what constituted a goal worth recapturing.

Hue was two cities, divided by the Perfume River. The old city on the north bank, the new French-built residential and administrative city on the south. One hundred and fifty years before Tet, the Emperor Gia Long had gotten French engineers to build a huge citadel in the north city and inside that an imperial palace fortress. It was into the fortress that the Tet invaders went after blowing up the bridge over the Perfume River which divided Hue into two cities. For over a week the battle raged, but for every shell and mortar fired by American troops, heavier fire was coming back. On the eleventh of February, having imported considerable forces, the Americans attacked across the river with helicopter gunships and assault boats, and successfully penetrated the citadel.

Leeming was in the third wave. He remembered the crossing in the boat, climbing through a breech in the wall, heading for the west wall and the Imperial Palace. But the firing was coming from everywhere. The VC were down in the myriad of cellars below the citadel, and had already burrowed tunnels under its main wall to bring in reinforcements under night cover. He recalled running down a narrow cobbled street, colliding head-on with a young SP4, a blond boy, face covered with blood. The boy had gone down in a scream but hadn't got up. Leeming had pulled him roughly to his feet, thinking the kid was running away. Then he saw that most of the boy's back had been blown away and he was dying. The boy kept shouting at him, "Incoming, incoming, man! Incoming!" warning Leeming of the now nonexistent mortar shell that had fatally wounded him.

"Where are you going?" Leeming had asked. There was no place safe for the boy to run with the all-directional VC fire.

"Grab some fifty-cal ammo. You go forward, Chief. They need some dudes in the first line. I lost my fucking pot [helmet], man! You go front, I'll get that fifty cal . . ."

Then the boy had leaned back against the citadel wall

and died. A bullet had hit Leeming in the chest, and as he'd collapsed, he'd pulled the dead boy over him, an unthought-through instinctual act to protect himself from other shots aimed or ricocheting down the alleyway. He'd received a bullet in the lung, something that would take six weeks of intensive care and six weeks of recuperation before he was well again. But he had not lost consciousness for hours after that shot.

He had lain there in the nightmare of the battle raging around him, thinking, then as now, about citadels and enemies in cellars. For a second time he was the victim of a citadel, or was it the same citadel? Maybe he had never gotten away from Hue. The nightmare of Hue had been the dead body of the boy on top of him. The body had started as a protective layer against ricochets and had ended as a ton-weight pressing down to flatten his broken chest, to asphyxiate him. Now in the farmhouse north of Scutari he felt that same weight crushing him again, but he couldn't identify it. He came out of deep unconsciousness and realized it had been nothing but the dream collecting and focusing every point of pain in his body.

He could hear Dhoc moving around the farmhouse. He heard a door scrape open and close and the squeak of a floorboard above him. He heard startled birds outside fly into the lowering sky, presumably at some appearance of the man in a window. "I know what he's waiting for," Leeming told himself—"It's his decision not to execute someone who's already dying. He's waiting to see if I die."

At one point he felt that if he held the M40, resting it on its butt, every time he drifted into unconsciousness the gun would fall over and make enough noise to awaken him. It didn't happen. He drifted once more into the screamless void of pain and awoke to find he still held the gun upright.

As an exercise in concentration, he tried dismantling the gun. The butt came away easily from the short stock and he could pull away the magazine. He put the gun aside and he realized now that he was sitting half-upright in a pool of his own fresh blood. There was a wound he hadn't known about, in his right thigh. He went down painfully on hands and knees and crawled ten feet past Buckman's body to the First Aid kit. Dragging the black box, he struggled back to take up the same position again, facing the door.

Opening the box, he saw the "Morphine," but knew it would automatically tip him into sleep. Van Dhoc would soon be in the room and he must lie ready, if only to die conscious and alert—not to have a bullet delivered into his comatose body. He picked out bandages and a bottle of something that looked like disinfectant. He tore off some bandage and made it into a small wad, poured the iodine substance on it and plugged it into the inch-deep hole in his thigh. The pain bulleted up his right side and he heard a scream so loud that for a moment he couldn't believe it came from his own mouth. He lost consciousness.

He came around and looked at his watch. It had stopped at four-fifty-seven. It was not yet totally black outside. Maybe seven—seven P.M. Why had Van Dhoc not made his move?

He heard a noise on the other side of the room, turned rapidly, but it was only the bubble of gastric gases rumbling up through Buckman's dead body and out his mouth.

Then he heard slow, deliberate footsteps crossing the room above him. The door closed and the footsteps came down the stone steps at the side of the covered courtyard. They stopped outside the room. Leeming tried, but the tension of the last seconds had released that minute drop too much of adrenalin and he passed out again.

When he awoke Van Dhoc was standing in front of him.

In any society he would be described as a good-looking man, a face almost patrician with sharp features and deep-brown eyes. He was dressed in a blue denim shirt, a blue wool donkey jacket, and baggy black linen trousers. He would be about five-foot-ten but his up-right stance made him look taller. He studied Leeming, eyes boring into him. In one hand he held a gray cardboard-covered folio. He was holding it loosely downward and Leeming could see it contained sheets of typescript, with photographs, passport size, stapled to the sheets. In his other hand he held a nine-millimeter Walther automatic.

Dhoc raised the gun and the folio. His thumb was already in position between pages. He opened the folio. There was a passport-sized photo on a page. He looked from the photo to Leeming and then dropped the folio onto the stone floor. "Colonel Leeming," he said, soft-voiced, gentle. Leeming found it hard to believe that voice could belong to Caswell's executioner.

Leeming said nothing, looked at the folio where it had fallen and spilled some pages across the floor. He was trying to read the writing on the cover. He'd seen folios like that before, in Vietnam. Dhoc had somehow gotten hold of the CIF investigation report into the events at Da Loc. Where had he gotten the file? In the chaos of the last fourteen days of the war, as the victorious NLA drove down Highway One heading for Saigon, all those papers were supposed to have been sent to the U.S.A. or burned or shredded.

"You speak English?" Leeming asked.

Dhoc looked him over, shrugged. "Three years learn, so I can find all of you. I not expect to find you in Albania."

"What do you want?" Leeming's voice low and mirroring his pain.

"You were the one who said Da Loc the village to raid," Van Dhoc announced. "I wanted you more than anyone."

Leeming saw something come into the man's eyes, an expression of white rage. The man was trembling, the hand on the Walther shaking as if he could not wait another second before using it.

"After Tet I sent in an intelligence report. Your people used many shells and mortar bombs, guns and ammunition in the offensive at Hue."

Van Dhoc leaned forward as Leeming's voice was sinking lower.

"Our people thought these huge quantities of arms, ordnance, were brought across country to Hue from the Ho Chi Minh trail. I knew they couldn't have been. I ran a Special Forces Camp, positioned on the route between the Ho Chi Minh trail and Hue. We were always patrolling the area. We saw no sign of huge shipments from the trail to Hue. Which could only mean one thing. Five miles to the east was the town of Da Loc, the only other town with easy access to Hue. I decided arms, explosives, mortars for the battle of Hue must have been hidden, slowly accumulated for months, maybe years, in Da Loc. That was the report I sent in, while I was wounded in the hospital, after the battle for Hue. I had no other involvement in the massacre at Da Loc."

Van Dhoc was shaking his head slowly. "Because of your report they went to Da Loc." He stopped for a moment, as if he could only control one function—either his voice or his emotions. Then he went on. "I was there, in secret cellar when your Army came. My wife was in the village with my children. They were murdered, all murdered."

"It was a tragic error and mistake."

"No error. No mistake." The Vietnamese voice sounded distant, hollow. "The destruction of Da Loc was given to men who would kill, and they did."

"It was a mistake in the madness of an insane war. Your people made these mistakes. There were the massacres done by your side. I saw them."

"There was no massacre like Da Loc. We had executions, many quislings and enemies of the people shot. You always forgot, didn't you, Vietnam was our country. You were the invaders. Those who helped you, the traitors."

Leeming felt the nausea of coming unconsciousness begin to sap his body again. He wanted an answer from

Dhoc before it was all over. "How did you get here? How did you survive the explosions?"

"I study the colonel general's body on the beach. I decide he tells you I am hid in citadel Scutari. I look out for you. I see you and your men arrive and investigate the diggings. I follow you. I did not think you could destroy the rocket installations. I would not think so few could do that. This afternoon I saw your preparations. I go to the rocket site, go down the tunnel, but come up minutes later in the citadel. I have binoculars. I saw you arrive. I thought I would execute you this afternoon. But then the explosions. I thought if somehow you lived, you would return here." There was silence a moment, then he gestured with the Walther toward Buckman's body. "Why," he asked softly, "did you shoot this one?"

"I killed him for his treachery."

"Treachery." Dhoc echoed the word. "Strange word from murderer of Da Loc. Where is the gun you shoot him with?" Dhoc's eyes searched the dusk shadows of the room.

"The gun is in this room," Leeming said. "Why shouldn't I use the word treachery? A word your people, I think more than ours, perfected in Vietnam."

Van Dhoc had gone over to the body of Buckman and with a foot turned it over. Underneath the body, where it had slipped from Buckman's shoulder holster, a Smith and Wesson. "You shot him with this?" Dhoc demanded.

"The worst treacheries I ever saw were the NLA's," Leeming said. He had to talk. He knew the effort of stringing the sentences together was the only thing keeping him conscious. "Once I was visiting a dressing station . . . south from the battle for Hue. They brought in a wounded VC. Not hurt bad . . . his leg broken . . . A splint had been put on it. The leg had been clumsily bandaged from top to bottom. Our doctors wanted to change this bandage but the man protested."

He was concentrating on the figure of Van Dhoc—the image of the man was beginning to swim. Dhoc had put down the Smith and Wesson and was staring at the five bullet holes in Buckman's chest, pensive. Leeming knew what the man was debating—were the large holes consistent with a .38 caliber wound?

". . . so the doctors left the VC alone. The reason the VC was protesting about the leg bandage being changed—he was waiting for an American soldier of high rank to come by. Late afternoon, a general arrived. The Viet Cong raised the bandaged leg and pointed it at the general, pulled the trigger. Under the bandage a hidden pistol. Our people had tried to give him medical aid and your man shot our general. I couldn't tolerate the treachery of allies, but between enemies like us it is the rule, Dhoc. That is war, nothing less, nor more, always . . ."

Dhoc was riveted there in the still half-crouched position over Buckman's body. He had made the connection between Leeming's story and the sight of the untidy bandages around Leeming's leg.

Leeming's finger found the trigger of the stockless M40 under the leg bandages, and he fired.

He lay back for a minute, pressing his head against the hard cold surface of the wall, and cried as Van Dhoc died.

The punch of the single shot from the M40 had thrown Dhoc back six feet and spun him flat to the ground, his face twisted away from Leeming. The bullet had gone straight through his chest at the level of his heart and passed out, leaving a hole, tennis-ball-size, low in the back of the donkey jacket. Leeming lay there and watched the blood pump out of the hole, first thickly, and then a minute later, as Van Dhoc's last soft breaths came, the blood became a trickle and stopped.

Leeming cried on. The act of killing had shattered him out of shock now and the full pain of his wounds was beginning to tear into him. And also he cried because Dhoc was dead and the ReKill on Da Loc was over.

He must now take the morphine if he was to survive. With the last energy in his body and with every nerve end jarring pain, he opened the First Aid box and took out four tablets. He crunched them slowly in his dry mouth. He had not completely swallowed them when the clouds entered his mind and spurred his pain to enter the black deep spiraling caves of unconsciousness again.

37

HE WOULD REMEMBER LITTLE of his last journey. Coming to in the moonlit room. Lighting a match that stirred some flies which had already sought the source of the room's smell and found the bodies. He remembered thinking how well the morphine had vanquished the worst of the pain, how quickly he had recovered some strength, until he tried to stand and found nothing to power his body upright, no reserves left. But he had stood, fallen, crawled across to the rubble heap, found a flashlight, come back to Van Dhoc's body, stiffening with the onset of rigor, moved it to find the rotor cap of the truck in one of his pockets. Then the memory became dimmer. The trip out to the truck, using muscles which were strings of pain, the crisis task of snapping the rotor cap back into place on the engine, the climb into the truck, and then the time spent sitting there with all hope draining out of him as the engine refused to start. It must have been on the last amp in the battery that the engine fired, and the nightmare of the journey up the Jezerce road to reference 404F began.

He had arrived over two hours late. Meyer had landed the Feiseler at the back of the power station at 2100. On his own initiative he'd waited. Meyer had approached the truck and Leeming had said one sentence. "Buckman is dead," then he'd slumped forward. He remembered nothing of the plane journey or anything else that happened till he awoke in an empty ward in the French Military Hospital in Belleville in the east of Paris three days later.

38

THE TUILERIES WERE UNFOLDING spring as dramati-
cally as any Verdi scene on stage in the place l'Opéra
building up the road. The daffodils were bursting out in
huge yellow swathes, the winter cherry sprinkling the
lawns with pink confetti, the gray trees coloring the first
fast shoots of lightest green along their branches. There
were crowds of people in the parks and on the pave-
ments, strolling off the claustrophobia of winter. And
Leeming was among them.

There had been a warm spell, Mackerras told him,
while he'd been away in Albania. Paris had had a lot of
days of sunshine. The general had waxed on about how
fine the weather had been—the sort of subject he was
happier expounding on after Leeming's first report. The
general wasn't too keen to discuss at length the Albanian mission and what exactly had happened.

Leeming had reported to him verbally from a hospital bed two days after arrival. Then four days later he'd
managed to dictate a statement which was typed and
which he signed. His report was accurate in all but one
detail. He'd written that Van Dhoc shot Buckman.
Mackerras questioned him about that several times.
How exactly it had happened, every detail. The general
had smelled a rat, and Leeming didn't understand why.
Unless he'd said something in the hearing of an orderly
or Mackerras, during the first days of delirium. Anyhow he stuck to the story.

His words at the first meeting with Mackerras had

been said coldly, acidly. "Wasn't the mission to kill Dhoc?"

"You did," Mackerras had replied. "You also destroyed a Chinese ballistic missile installation, as a side order to the main meal. A tremendous achievement."

"You miss the point," Leeming had said. "If you and Buckman had told us that site was going to blow high, six people could have lived."

"That was accidental."

"It wasn't," Leeming had said quietly. "It was murder."

"Careful, Colonel," Mackerras had warned.

At the second meeting, after he had dictated and signed his statement, the general asked if there was anything he wanted.

"Yes," Leeming had replied. "I'd like to see a girl. Her name's Lara. I don't even have her surname. I have her address."

"May I ask who she is?"

"She was Caswell's girl. She knew nothing of his mission, our mission. I'd like to see her."

She came to the hospital. The meeting was awkward. She had sat and held his hand. He was deliberately offhand with her about his scars and bandages.

She stayed only half an hour and was just leaving when he asked whether she could do something very important for him. She said yes. He asked her to hire a typewriter, put it in her apartment and find a firm that would photocopy the report he was going to write.

She kissed him on the forehead, left the room obviously depressed by his cool reception.

He remained in Belleville. The days passed monotonously as he picked up his strength. He could measure the increase in his physical well-being every afternoon when he took a stroll in the company of one of the hospital's male nurses through the Tuileries. On the seventh day after Lara's visit he was released from the hospital and told to go to the George V where a suite had been booked in his name. He was to wait for a call from Mackerras.

He took a cab directly to Lara's apartment in the rue de Duras. It was midmorning. He worked on his new report at the typewriter until midafternoon. She took it out and had five copies made. Each of the copies was then put in an envelope and addressed to one of the five generals whom Leeming knew took part in the original Pentagon meeting. They were General Harris, General Reiner—Intelligence G2 of Army Staff, Fort Wesley, General Bedale of Army Intelligence Corps Command, Fort Holabird, General Patterson—special assistant to the Chief of Staff Warfare Activities, and General Leimnitz—Chief of Army Intelligence Eastern Command.

The report began, "It is important to me that all of you are made aware, if you're not already, of the complete story of the Mackerras initiative in Albania." He had then gone on to detail the whole story, including the fact he had killed Buckman. He kept the story as brief as possible but still it ran to fifteen pages. He finished with two paragraphs.

"It's now clear to me that this mission to Albania was too complex in plan and execution to have been an Army G2 initiative. Buckman, I know, sincerely believed that it was, boasted proudly that this mission was going to put G2 firmly back on the map, and as a by-product save it from being taken over by the CIA.

"I believe Buckman was always deluded. I think this plot has all the hallmarks of the CIA. I'm not clear whether you know the obvious, are party to the obvious, or ignorant of the obvious. I believe that Army Intelligence has been, or is in the process of being absorbed by the Central Intelligence Agency, and that General Mackerras is a member of that agency. Out of respect for those who gave their lives I write this latest report. If these facts are known to you, my words are pointless. If not, then perhaps it is not too late for you to take the appropriate action."

Lara went off and posted the five envelopes. The writing, duplicating and posting of the letters was all completed by six o'clock.

She could see when she returned to the apartment that a load seemed to have lifted from his shoulders. She asked him if he would join her for a light dinner in the apartment.

He said yes.

She said she would have to go down the road to the market to buy some provisions for the meal.

He said he'd head off the other way, for a short convalescent stroll up to the Seine and across to the Tuileries.

When he left, he gave her a little kiss on the forehead but no smile. As he walked north up the rue de Duras he noticed the man across the street waited until he was fifty yards away from the apartment before beginning to follow him.

He was a big man, over six feet, broadly built, with a new Burberry raincoat several sizes too large for him. Leeming had given the garment a long look. It had two flaps coming over the shoulders and buttoning midway down the chest. The bulge of a gun in a shoulder holster wouldn't be noticeable. In fact a complete arsenal, giving the man a real choice of weapons to kill Leeming, could easily be hidden under the folds of the oversize coat.

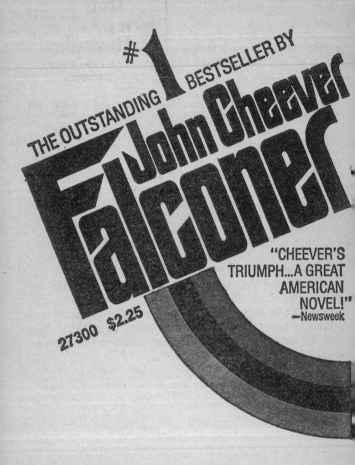

NEW FROM BALLANTINE!

FALCONER, John Cheever   27300 $2.25
The unforgettable story of a substantial, middle-class man and the passions that propel him into murder, prison, and an undreamed-of liberation. "CHEEVER'S TRIUMPH...A GREAT AMERICAN NOVEL."—*Newsweek*

GOODBYE, W. H. Manville   27118 $2.25
What happens when a woman turns a sexual fantasy into a fatal reality? The erotic thriller of the year! "Powerful."—*Village Voice.* "Hypnotic."—*Cosmopolitan.*

THE CAMERA NEVER BLINKS, Dan Rather
with Mickey Herskowitz   27423 $2.25
In this candid book, the co-editor of "60 Minutes" sketches vivid portraits of numerous personalities including JFK, LBJ and Nixon, and discusses his famous colleagues.

THE DRAGONS OF EDEN, Carl Sagan 26031 $2.25
An exciting and witty exploration of mankind's intelligence from pre-recorded time to the fantasy of a future race, by America's most appealing scientific spokesman.

VALENTINA, Fern Michaels   26011 $1.95
Sold into slavery in the Third Crusade, Valentina becomes a queen, only to find herself a slave to love.

THE BLACK DEATH, Gwyneth Cravens
and John S. Marr   27155 $2.50
A totally plausible novel of the panic that strikes when the bubonic plague devastates New York.

THE FLOWER OF THE STORM,
Beatrice Coogan   27368 $2.50
Love, pride and high drama set against the turbulent background of 19th century Ireland as a beautiful young woman fights for her inheritance and the man she loves.

THE JUDGMENT OF DEKE HUNTER,
George V. Higgins   25862 $1.95
Tough, dirty, shrewd, telling! "The best novel Higgins has written. Deke Hunter should have as many friends as Eddie Coyle."—*Kirkus Reviews*

LG-2